MARATHON
Looks on the Sea

MARATHON
Looks on the Sea

OLIVIA COOLIDGE

Pictures by Erwin Schachner

1967

HOUGHTON MIFFLIN COMPANY BOSTON

Books by Olivia Coolidge

Greek Myths

Legends of the North

The Trojan War

Egyptian Adventures

Cromwell's Head

Roman People

*Winston Churchill and the Story
of Two World Wars*

Caesar's Gallic War

Men of Athens

Makers of the Red Revolution

People in Palestine

Lives of Famous Romans

The King of Men

Marathon Looks on the Sea

CONTENTS

Introduction

Introduction

THE STORY of the Athenian victory at Marathon has been too simply told because it is symbolic. If it did not represent wide issues to us, we could dismiss it as a piece of border fighting that did not even settle the future of Athens, which was not at the time especially distinguished. In this way, certainly, the Persians regarded it. To us, however, the loss of Athenian civilization in the century which followed would have been irreparable. We sum up Marathon not in terms of what it was but of what we know came after.

This view of the affair may do for history, but it leaves fiction with little to say. Because the aftermath means more to us than the background, we are judging the battle without ever picturing the actual issues which were involved in it. Yet the storyteller cannot dismiss the Persians, ignore the tyrants, and treat Athens as though she were something she has not yet become. The battle of Marathon is part of a complex of events which includes the campaigns of Darius, the rebellion and destruction of Miletos, the ambitions of Miltiades in the north, the expulsion of the tyrants, and the rivalries of countless little states.

Such complication presents the novelist with a considerable challenge, not only in itself but because the reader has been previously led to expect that Marathon is simple. Actually, events are scattered widely in distance and time during a period when unity was the last thing that anyone, except, of course, the Persians, ever wanted. The story of Miltiades, both what we know and what we can guess, is dramatic. But it is not unified in time. His operations in the Chersonese must have lasted about thirty years. Similarly the rise of democracy is of vital importance, but it is not unified in place, since it happened all over the Aegean Sea. The attempts of Darius to extend his empire go on steadily from 514 B.C. or so until 490 B.C.

Drastic simplification is as necessary to the novelist as to the general historian; but it cannot be the same. A story cannot take into account what has not yet happened. The battle of Marathon becomes a conflict not between tyranny and liberty, but between two civilizations, each commanding the loyalty and love of superior people. If our hero is not placed in a position where he is really torn between them, we have been unfair to one side or the other. He chooses, of course, the people he really belongs to; but many he loves and admires are ranged against him.

Both novelist and historian are trying to make their issues plain without conflicting with what they see as historical truth. A small example of the constant difficulties which arise is my confusing use of the word "tyrant" to describe what is in modern terms quite simply a dictator. Unfortunately "dictator" is a Roman word which has not been invented at the period I write of, so that even at the risk of muddling readers, I cannot use it to designate a tyrant. But I have no special scruples about jumping over years or omitting events which I do not think important to my story. Even historians as a matter of course must do the same.

We are not historians, however, we novelists. Battles may be significant, but they are also exciting. People have adventures, make decisions, love as vividly in the distant past as they do in the present. We are putting on a show, not merely summing up an era. We are writing about something we have felt, not simply studied. History to us is not only a rigid set of facts. It is sensation, action, life, love, suffering. It leaps, it lingers; above all, it makes stories. History is the life of people.

The Summons

Miltiades, son of Cimon, galloped madly across the plain of Marathon down to the sea. He rode without saddle or stirrups so that nothing but the grip of his bare brown knees kept him from bouncing high into the air at every stride and dropping back with a teeth-jarring crash. The wind, streaming past him, fluttered his blue cloak out behind and ruffled his hair into thick black curls standing up from his forehead.

It was early morning, and the sun peeped up across the jagged island of Euboea to make a glittering path across the narrow sea. It shone full in Miltiades's eyes, so that he kept them cast down on the ground. Actually, he needed to watch his path because the stony track went zig-zagging across the plain between the boundary stones of his neighbors, whose land hunger impelled them to encroach on it, here by a foot and there by a yard.

He thundered past the stone wall which fenced his own vineyard, in which two of his farm servants were already working. They stopped to watch him go, leaning on their hoes.

"He'll break his neck some day," growled one with a shake of the head.

"Anyone else would, but not he," retorted the other.

Miltiades swerved as the path curved suddenly round a sacred olive tree, hollow and half dead, but still showing green at the end of a few branches. His horse slipped sideways, skidding on loose stones, but in a second he was around again and tearing over rough pasture which, since it was his own, provided a short cut.

He was riding as though his life depended on speed; and yet there was no reason for his hurry, save that it satisfied his nervous energies. His boat should not be back from Euboea much before noon; and though he depended on his cousin there to pass on messages which came from the outer world, these were seldom important. He had nothing to do on the coast while he waited, except to examine the shrine of Hercules, a tiny wooden building in a grove on a small mound at the south end of the plain. He kept it in repair because he was the wealthiest landowner in these parts, and also because he envied Hercules with passion. What toils that hero had undergone! What places and people he had visited! What glory he had won! Miltiades dug his heels impatiently into his mare's ribs and urged her on.

What use to envy Hercules when he dared not so much as visit Athens twenty miles off? Miltiades had the sense to see that it would profit nothing to be mysteriously murdered, as his father Cimon had been. No accusations had been made about old Cimon's death; but it was plain that his fault, if any, had lain in being fabulously wealthy and in owning the mares which had set a record by winning the chariot race at Olympia three times running. Hippias, the tyrant of Athens, fixed the gaze of suspicion on all who were too much in the public eye. Miltiades had seen the need to keep out of Hippias's sight. He had retired to the Marathon farm and must needs get his excitement by galloping like a madman over the plain.

He blinked at the glittering sea and thought he saw something which caused him to jerk at the reins and pull up in a shower of pebbles. He shaded his eyes with his hand and peered for a moment. He had been right! A boat was putting in. This was an extraordinary thing, since it must have left Euboea long before the sun was up. Nobody ever sailed at night, save in emergency.

Sobered, he set his horse to a walk. There was plenty of time to get down to the beach before it arrived. Gulls were flying, uttering their shrill screech which sounded almost like the cries of wounded men after a great battle.

Idly and with one part of his mind he reflected that this was always a place of echoes. Strange that so dull and familiar a spot as Marathon plain should have a reputation for being haunted! Miltiades brooded over the subject because he was trying to hold down consuming impatience. No message that he might reasonably expect would be of importance to himself. Most probably the cousin in Euboea or the brother who had the luck to inherit the family position in the distant Chersonese wanted advice on how to deal with Hippias of Athens.

Miltiades tethered his horse to a convenient bush and walked down to the beach, a stocky figure burned brown by twenty-five hot summers, barefoot, and clad in a tunic of unbleached wool like any poor farmer. His cloak he had left on the mare because she was sweaty.

They saw him from the boat and waved, altering course to beach her where he stood. With a stir of interest he saw that she had strangers aboard, one gray-haired and clad in a long gown, the other an active-looking man with a sword at his girdle. They were standing in the prow to stare at him, but they did not call a greeting, contenting themselves with raising a hand as the crew leaped into the shallows to heave the boat above the water line. The younger man vaulted over the side, while the elder waited for a plank to be put out and descended with cautious dignity. Not until he was safely on dry land did both of them turn to Miltiades. Even then it almost seemed as though the elder, though he clearly was the spokesman, had nothing to say. He ran his tongue across his lips and swallowed.

"My lord . . . Miltiades."

Miltiades raised his dark eyebrows, but said nothing. He was master to his slaves, but lord to no man; and he did not know how to answer such a title.

The old man fumbled with a string which secured something about his neck. He undid it and put the object in Miltiades's hand.

It was a seal ring with a dull red stone in which the hand of a master had graven a tiny chariot and horses. Miltiades turned it over. He had never seen it before, but he knew its impression well enough. He had seen that a hundred times in wax on letters from his brother, who had the luck to rule a trading outpost at the entrance of the Black Sea, while he, Miltiades, ate his heart out doing nothing outside Athens.

He looked at the ring for a long, still moment, hardly thinking because he did not dare to think. The gulls flew over crying their strange scream, and he listened to them. Eventually he lifted his eyes and said, "My brother?"

The younger man pushed forward impatiently. "Your brother is dead, my lord, and all the Chersonese is in rebellion. Your inheritance can be lost by delay of a day, even of an hour. It might be saved for you by the chance that you stood on the strand as we came in and were not a few miles off in Marathon. Minutes are wasting while we stand idly here. Come with us if you will strike a blow for what is yours."

Miltiades closed his hand on the ring. He felt no personal sorrow for his brother, whom he had not seen since he was five years old, but he was awed by the suddenness with which death had come upon him. He turned to the older man. "Was he killed in battle?" He was well aware that the five little cities which his brother had ruled in the barren Chersonese were no more than trading stations always subject to raids by the natives of the hinterland. Indeed, it was only by virtue of a gift for soldiering that his family had become rulers in the first place.

"It was a conspiracy, Lord," the elder said. "As your brother sat on his throne judging a case, one of the complainants rushed upon him, while the other and his supporters killed the guards. Now rebellion gathers way because our party has no leader, and it is true that there is not an hour to be lost."

Miltiades smiled grimly. Impetuous he might be when there was nothing important to be done, but in emergency he was cool and slippery as ice. "The gods may grant us half an hour," he said. Nothing would induce him to rush away with people whose names and position he did not know to put down a rebellion about whose causes and supporters he was ignorant. The younger man grunted impatiently at his questions; but the elder was ready to tell all he knew, which was not much. He had been a week on the voyage, and the position in the Chersonese was greatly confused when he left. Anything might have happened.

"And you think I will set out with you in that cockle shell," said Miltiades hotly, "which may quite likely take ten days to return if winds are adverse. You will put me ashore as I am, without followers or armor. If this is your judgment, then it is small wonder that rebels gain ground in the Chersonese. Hippias of Athens has ships which will beat yours by a week, and Hippias knows that it is to his advantage that the mouth of the Black Sea be held by an Athenian. Turn yourselves about and start for home! I travel too fast to take you with me."

He wasted no further time in argument, but turned his back on them to run up the beach and was away in a thunder of hooves, adventure before him and the echoing shore with its screeching gulls behind.

Miltiades rode into the courtyard of his farm and tossed his reins to the chief groom as he sprang off. "Bridle me the big black horse and hold him ready. I'm riding to Athens. Andrios!"

"Master!" His personal servant had been lurking in the doorway in case he was wanted.

"My scarlet cloak with the golden brooch. It's heavier than this one, and nights will still be cool in the north. I'm going campaigning. There's armor in the house at Athens, isn't there? But bring me my sword."

Andrios blinked but recovered himself in a flash. "Shall they bridle the brown horse too? You'll need attendance."

Miltiades looked at his servant a little sadly. Andrios, who had served his father before him, was a graybeard, long unused to rugged conditions. He shook his head. "Not this time, Andrios. I'm off to the Chersonese. My brother's dead."

Andrios looked sour, which was his way of expressing hurt feelings. Miltiades attempted to console him. "I shall need you to bring me my wife and son as soon as it is safe. How can Leucippe, who has never been out of doors alone, travel north to meet me unless I leave you here to smooth her way?"

Andrios pursed his lips, but at least he vanished to carry out the orders he had been given. Following on his heels, Miltiades met his wife hurrying across the inner courtyard which connected the rooms of the main house with the women's quarters. Someone had rushed to her with the news, so that she flung herself into her husband's arms, heedless of who might be looking.

Miltiades was not so forgetful of dignity, but he patted Leucippe and let her cling to him. She was a tall woman with an abundance of yellow-brown hair, her greatest beauty. Her face was long and bony; and her teeth, though regular, were larger than they ought to be and rather yellow. She was a cousin to Hippias, so that Cimon in arranging the match had thought to protect himself by alliance with the tyrant. Though he had miscalculated in this, Leucippe had been an affectionate wife and had born a son. Unluckily she was in one of her hysterical moods when words of reason made no impression. In vain did Miltiades point out that the mulecart in which she traveled, her maids, her child, her nurse, her escort would take all day upon the road to Athens. Furthermore, the wagons would first have to be loaded with the treasure which they could not leave behind with the rough farm servants. Finally it was impossible that he should set sail with a train of women when fighting lay ahead. He would send for her as soon as he was able.

Leucippe listened only to protest. She did not need more than two women, one for herself and one for the boy. The business of moving the treasure could be done by Andrios as well as by her. Miltiades need not imagine that she who came of royal blood was frightened of war.

Miltiades disengaged her arms from his neck, stepping backwards to exchange his cloak for the scarlet one which Andrios brought him. "Where's the boy?" he asked to cut off complaints from Leucippe.

Andrios did not know, but he had sent slaves looking for him. The child was six years old, too big for his nurse and brimful of mischief. Miltiades smiled as he buckled his sword, but he was angry that Leucippe did not keep her brat under better control. It hurt him to go without seeing the boy, but he must not delay.

He went out into the yard with hasty strides, lest Leucippe try to take him in her arms again. Parting was hard enough without making such a clamor. He was glad to see that the boy was there after all, dodging about the horse and getting in the groom's way. He was a black-haired imp, clad in nothing but a liberal coat of dirt and a little amulet against the evil eye. Miltiades took him in his arms to toss him high into the air and catch him again. He squealed with excitement.

"Take me to Athens with you on your horse! Take me to Athens!"

Miltiades laughed. "I'm going further than Athens, and you shall come when you can catch me up."

"I'll catch you," the imp said. He grabbed his father around the knee. "I've got you. I'll keep you."

Miltiades plucked the boy loose and lifted him above his head, where he held him wriggling for a moment. Lowering his arms, he tossed him lightly to Andrios. "Catch me if you can!" He vaulted onto the horse's back, seized the reins, and was off like a thunderbolt without looking back. Andrios and the boy watched the scarlet cloak grow smaller and disappear in a clump of olive trees.

Leucippe ran out into the yard. There were tears on her sallow cheeks and her long fingers trembled. Her voice was sharp. "Andrios! Tell the men to harness my mules. And nurse — where's nurse? Let her wash the boy and put on his tunic. We're going to Athens. Hurry! Hurry!"

The First Escape

Leucippe had thrown herself down on her marriage bed to cry her heart out. The train of servants with which she had rushed to Athens had gathered for a gossip in the central court of the house, neglectful of its dust and disarray. The urgency with which Leucippe had hurried them all, frantic to overtake her husband, had prevented them from discussing matters which concerned their own futures as well as those of their masters.

"He was sent off in a ship of war with fifty oars," exclaimed the porter. "Their orders were not to stop overnight or cook ashore. The rowers, all picked men, are to be kept going by bread dipped in wine and thrust into their mouths while they are swinging."

"They crowded the gangways with extras to relieve them," added the sub-porter, who had slipped out to gather news and had been gone several hours. "The tyrant Hippias rode down to the bay himself to see to it."

"Bodyguard and all," agreed the porter.

"Hippias knows how to act with speed," approved Andrios, "where his own interests are involved. The Chersonese controls the Black Sea trade, which is vital to Athens."

People nodded wisely. Such statesmanlike words put the porters in their place. They were rough-looking servants whose duty it was to remain silent until more valuable slaves had opened their mouths. It happened, however, that the two of them had acted as watchmen in the closed house, so that they had opened to the master when he came storming in. Miltiades had come like a whirlwind and left in the same hurry, never staying for the arrival of his wife, whom he thought in Marathon.

"The mistress, after all, is Hippias's cousin," reminded Leucippe's personal maid, who had come with her mistress from her childhood home and expected in Miltiades's absence to be ruler of the household. "Our tyrant must surely desire to see her a queen."

Andrios stroked his beard in a doubtful gesture. Little good had the master's connection with Hippias done old

Cimon! Little good had it done Miltiades until now! Leucippe, who like all married women never went out and who spoke to no free man except her husband, could hardly be an object of personal affection to the tyrant. Still kin was kin and must be reckoned with. It was just possible the personal maid was right.

"I told you so!" cried the child's nurse, whose rivalry with the maid was becoming desperate because the boy was nearly old enough to be taken out of women's hands. "Did I not mention how I saw three crows in our great oak? I am so sensitive that I always know beforehand of bad tidings."

"If you can call it bad tidings," retorted the personal maid with a sniff, "to inherit a kingdom."

"Not a kingdom!" Andrios wrinkled his brow with gloomy foreboding. "If it were a true kingdom, then Miltiades might hope to die in his bed. But look at Hippias with his foreign guard, his dark suspicions, his secret assassins. A tyrant rules by force; and be he good or bad, by force he dies. I fear for the master."

The nurse gave an affected scream, but her heart was not in it. She was bound to remember that the heir was peculiarly her own. The maid, giving her a glance of contempt, reminded Andrios that the family had been invited to rule the Chersonese. They had not imposed themselves, as had the Athenian tyrants, on unwilling people.

"There are always some unwilling," Andrios pointed out. "How do you imagine our master's brother died?"

The porter gave an indignant glance at Andrios, for this piece of information had been gleaned by the sub-porter from the gossip of the Athenian streets. But Andrios was not to be put down by any cheap slave. He looked around him, gathering the general attention. "Where's the boy?" he asked, suddenly cautious.

"With his mother," answered the nurse, impatient for sensation. "Tell us, Andrios."

"He was cut down," said Andrios, lowering his voice with relish, "in his own throne room by one of his own subjects . . . with an axe."

The nurse screamed, this time more loudly.

"And all the Chersonese is up in arms," Andrios told them. "Why did you think Miltiades left in such a hurry?"

Leucippe's maid, who had sacrificed this tidbit of news to her desire to make trouble for the nurse, came hurrying back through a doorway, her wrinkled face set in smug satisfaction. "Is it not your duty, nurse, to look after the boy? He is not with his mother."

There had been no porter at the door and no one's watchful eye on what he was doing when the boy crept quietly out. He knew that the grownups would hustle him back and slap him if they caught him, but he was used to thinking faster than they did and getting his own way. Fortune favored his attempt. Athenian houses presented blank walls to the street, which was by chance empty. The bustle of the day started early and was already over. Athenians had gone to exercise, or at least watch others do so. It was the year of the great games at Delphi, so that the form of Athenian athletes was a matter of city-wide interest. There were also choruses training for competition in a festival which the tyrant had enlarged. On

the Acropolis rock, the first section of painted statuary
had just been hoisted into place on the façade of the tyrant's new temple. It must be viewed and discussed
without delay. Such things were important. In fact, there
was plenty to do or see without bothering about a little
boy running down a dusty street to get out of sight.

Thinking only of escape, the child turned a couple of
corners before he slowed his pace, awed by the comparative
bustle of a street where commercial activities were still
going on. It is true that the hours of buying and selling
were over, but shops stood open; and slaves, who had no
hours off, were busy in them manufacturing the sandals
and leatherwork which were the staples of the district. A
free man would have stopped the boy, for it was never in
the nature of Athenians to mind their own business.
Slaves, however, were unwilling to interfere in the affairs
of the freeborn. They merely vented their curiosity by
calling out to one another. "Ever see that child before?
There's one who escaped from his nurse!"

"Escaped!" rang alarmingly in the boy's ears. There
were people walking the street, slaves in working tunics
out on errands. Used to the farm, where all the servants
knew him and every adult joined in a conspiracy to keep
him from doing what he wanted, the boy felt panic. Hastily
he dived down an alley, rubbish-strewn and evil-smell-
ing, but at least dark and quiet. As he paused to get his
breath, it suddenly came over him that he did not know
where he was or in what direction he ought to be going.

Tears came into his eyes, but he blinked them back.
His magnificent father had said the great thing was never

to give up. He knew this warren of streets would not go on forever, since he had come into town this morning from the country. He had asked then where his father would take ship. They had told him, pointing out landmarks with careful gestures but omitting to mention that the harbor was three good miles from the city of Athens. He had not learned about Miltiades's sailing, since Leucippe had been sure she would catch up with her husband.

He did not want to face the streets again, but in the alley the buildings were so close together that he could see nothing but a strip of sky. Until the Acropolis rock, towering high above the city, came to light, he could make no sort of guess at his direction.

"Hurry! Hurry!" Leucippe had been urging on the carts all the way, frantic to reach the town, vainly imagining that her husband might take her after all, despite the urgency, the distance, and the danger. The boy, too, was more afraid of being left behind than he was of the noisy streets, so that with reluctant feet he picked his way past garbage to the alley's end, sidled quietly into a wider street, and stood looking about him.

A hand fell on his shoulder from behind. "Hey, boy! Lost your mother?"

The boy gave a great tug and tried to squirm free. He was swung around violently and found himself facing a lean, brown man with a crooked nose and a pair of alert eyes set close together.

"Let me go! Let me go to my father!" The boy, who was expert at making escape from his elders, gave another wriggle which nearly caught his captor off guard. But all he got for his pains was a clout on the ear which made his head sing. "Stand still, you little rat! Where is your father?"

"He's on a ship," the boy said sullenly.

"A ship! Oho!" The stranger whistled thoughtfully through a gap in his front teeth as though this answer put a fresh complexion on the matter, as indeed from his point of view it did. He looked the boy over with interest. The child was grubby, as boys of six or seven always will be. But he wore a tunic, whereas most boys of pre-school age wore little or nothing. His dark hair, not yet cut, hung over his shoulders in tangled curls, faintly smelling of perfume. His amulet against the evil eye hung not from a strip of leather, but from a worked chain like that of a rich man's son. In fact, the boy looked like treasure trove. The only question was how to make the largest profit from him.

The safe and sensible thing was to restore him to his family, which must be looking for him. But then rich men in his experience were mean. The moment they saw his worn brown cloak and battered features, they would think a single piece of silver good enough for a man who had rescued their hopeful son from a fate worse than death. On the other hand in a foreign port men would pay good money for a slave as handsome as this child and already of a teachable age.

There was a long silence. The boy was simply waiting for the grip on his arm to relax so that he could make another bid for freedom. The shabby man was thinking things over.

His need for money was urgent. He was not a brigand, but he had lived too hard a life to have many scruples. It might be possible not to sell the boy, but hold him for ransom. On the other hand, there would be certain dangers in walking with the child through town, where either of them might be recognized. In any case, their association would look odd. He did not flatter himself that he resembled the respectable tutor who ought to be at this child's heels. Athenians, busybodies to a man, would certainly gossip. If the child disappeared, Athens would become too hot to hold him.

It was a weakness of the shabby man's to like a risk. If stopped on the way to the docks, he was only escorting the child to where he said he belonged. When they got there, he would still be able to choose whether he would deliver the boy to his father or ship him with a crony of his own, who would sell him in Cyprus.

He nodded, making up his mind. "On a ship? A lucky chance! I am going down to the docks myself and can take you with me."

It was the boy's turn to hesitate now. Fresh from the country, he was not aware that city strangers might be evil. Nor did the dirty tunic and patched cloak of his new friend look worse than working costumes he was used to on the farm. But a grownup willing to aid and abet him was quite novel.

"Ah well, if you know your own way," said the shabby man shrewdly. "I daresay you want no help in your adventure."

The boy's face lighted up with triumphant glee. "It *is* an adventure!"

The shabby man, who had seen many ports and all manner of people, looked down into the dancing eyes with a sense of shock. The expression in them had gleamed in his own face when he had been younger, less soured and cynical. The boy was alive with the excitement of the born adventurer who will court danger because he enjoys it. "You were frightened when you came out of that alley," he said, certain that this was so and that the sensation had merely added a fillip to running away. The child nodded, silently nursing exhilaration.

He let the boy go and turned away sharply. "This way," he said, uncertain whether the child would follow and also whether he desired him to do so. He had seen too much for pity to move him, but the realization that they were two of a kind made him uncomfortable. He knew how such a spirit would batter itself to death in slavery.

He did not look around, but he heard the boy follow. "Well then, so be it," he said to himself. But aloud he said, "My business demands haste, so that if you cannot keep up . . ."

Without answering, the boy broke into a trot. Well-grown for his age and hard as nails, he looked as though he would be difficult to shake off. The shabby man soon slackened his pace. No need for decisions about what to do till they got out of Athens.

They were keeping to the narrow streets as they made a detour around the market, which would, in the shabby man's view, be dangerous crossing. This was the center of town and never deserted by loiterers looking for something to gossip about. But the market extended itself here and there into smaller open spaces where two or three narrow streets met and where the river of country traffic which flowed daily into the city would back up in a milling crowd of goats and donkeys with their perspiring drovers. It was notable that the pace of the shabby man increased as they crossed such clearings, and that he glanced about him before deserting the safety of walls. But Hermes, who is god of thieves, was not with him.

"Cleophon, my dear old friend! Well met in Athens! So you did escape from Ephesus alive! I thought you in Hades."

"Cleon, not Cleophon, you fool! And keep your voice down!" The shabby man, fairly caught in the open, frowned at his dear old friend and gestured angrily at the other side of the little square, where a group of barbarian soldiers with swords at their sides was loitering around a door which differed from other house doors in Athens, not in size or importance, but in being open.

"Cleon if you will," agreed the other amiably. "When I was younger and went on my travels, I knew a Cleophon who was not afraid to meddle in political matters. The Persian governor set a price on his head and had him hunted through all the Greek cities of the coast. He might have caught him for all I ever heard. Or possibly Cleophon adopted a new name. Here in Athens he may call himself what he pleases and come to no harm. We do not take account of who governs in Sardis."

"More fools you!" growled Cleon with a vehemence which caused a couple of passers-by to stop and listen. Athenians were always curious.

His acquaintance, a stout, respectable person neatly barbered, looked uneasy. He had forgotten when he stopped to greet his old friend that an exile with a grievance might be an awkward man to know. One was never sure what secret informers Hippias had in his pay or what change of policy might focus the Athenian tyrant's dark suspicions on new people.

"Is that your boy?" he asked, swiftly turning conversation into a harmless channel while he watched the passers-by lounge on. "A handsome son! What's your name, boy?"

"Metiochos, son of Miltiades," replied the child proudly.

"Metiochos, son of . . ." It took the Athenian a minute to take in a truth so unexpected that at first he could not believe it. He put a hand on Cleon's arm as though to steady himself while he stared down at the child. "But . . . but . . . I watched Miltiades ride down to the harbor with the tyrant. Black eyes he has, black hair and beard. That cock of the head! Son of Miltiades! By Zeus, he *is*."

"I found him in a street nearby," Cleon muttered. The son of Miltiades was far too important for him to meddle with. Besides, this friend of his youth, this Euphorion, knew his real name. He did not want to be surrendered to the Persian.

"He is taking me down to the harbor to my father," put

in the boy, anxious to cut short further inquiries. "On a ship. We have to hurry."

"On a ship!" Euphorion turned angrily on his dear old friend. "What's your game with the boy, eh? You know Miltiades has sailed already."

The boy's eyes filled, and a big tear rolled down his cheek; but he shook his head, dumbly denying the news. The two grownups were paying no attention to his dismay. Euphorion had tightened his grip on Cleon's arm. "If I thought you had intended . . . By Zeus, if I thought that! Have you sunk to brigandage?"

"Don't be foolish," Cleon had begun when the boy, perceiving that both of the men had turned against him, was away like a startled rabbit.

"Hey, stop! Stop him, you there!" Euphorion, who had hopeful sons of his own, understood the dangers which might lurk in the streets of a city. He gave chase. Cleon, more prudently, faded into an alley to watch events.

The boy was agile, while Euphorion was short-legged and growing tubby. All the same, the child would have had no chance, had not a couple of young men, coming back from exercise and ready for mischief, planted themselves in Euphorion's way. By the time he had swerved around them, the boy had started down an alley, changed his mind as he saw people in it, and dodged back. Running full tilt with Euphorion close behind him, he made for the marketplace, where quantities of small wicker booths might serve to hide him. The two young athletes, joined by other loungers, cheered him on. The guards of Hippias, who might easily have stopped him, laid bets on the winner.

On this side of the square, the house of Hippias formed part of a huddle of buildings which narrowed the entrance to the marketplace. Out of the market were emerging a half dozen fresh guards, surrounding the figure of Hippias's eldest grandson, who was returning from the exercise ground with his tutor in attendance.

His family was as dear to Hippias as his own life, which he had guarded with ever-increasing care since the death of his father. He clearly understood that a dictatorship which lasted into the second generation lost its charm. Thus on the one hand he courted popularity through the splendor of his buildings and the elaboration of his public festivals. On the other hand, he increased the numbers of his barbarian guards and gave them stringent orders. Trouble soon arose between them and the populace, which made him ever more nervous. It was decreed by now that no one might press too close to the soldiers as they guarded their masters through the streets, their hands on their swords. Thus when Metiochos, running head down, charged into them around the corner, he was met by a violent thrust from a startled soldier which sent him literally flying. His head went back against the wall with an audible thump, and he collapsed limply.

There was an instant's shocked silence in the square, where little groups of men had been idly grinning. Euphorion bent over the boy and raised him up, head hanging.

"Murderers!" It was Cleon's voice that raised the first cry as he sent a stone whizzing. But the two young athletes did not hold back, and their example was rapidly followed. More Athenians, swarming as was their custom to the scene of excitement, joined in with furious cries against the soldiers.

"Murderers! Assassins! Barbarians!" Few of the people who rushed onto the scene knew the cause of the riot, but everyone was eager to pelt the soldiers, while stones were plentiful in Athens.

"Down with the tyrant!" shouted one. "Democracy!" yelled another, raising the latest battle cry of the common people.

The soldiers, drawing together, made little rushes at the crowd, which scattered screaming and reformed when they retreated. Pisistratos, the tyrant's youthful grandson, had a cut on his forehead and clung to his tutor, white as a sheet. His escort had placed him close against the wall and were trying to edge him into safety amid a hail of brickbats.

"The archers! The archers!" The moment that cry was raised, the square began to empty far faster than it had filled up. Everybody knew the tyrant's archers were not afraid to shoot, and no one wished to be killed as an example to the restive populace. In a couple of minutes there was no one to be seen but Euphorion, who, burdened by the boy, had taken refuge from ill-aimed missiles in a corner of the buildings.

"That's the man!" cried the tyrant's grandson in a high, shrill voice. "He started the riot."

A couple of soldiers seized Euphorion. He, however, retaining his presence of mind, cried out loudly that he had started nothing. What was more, he was a decent citizen from the district of Eleusis and well connected. Half a dozen worthies there would vouch for him as being none of your stone-throwing riffraff. Was he at fault because he had gone to the rescue of a boy who was close kin to Hippias? They had better be careful what they did to him.

The captain of the guard, who was just a barbarian like all the rest and had no authority to bully citizens of note, was taken aback. The name of Miltiades, which Euphorion did not fail to pronounce in threatening tones, frightened him further. In fact, he neither dared let Euphorion go nor arrest him. He compromised by telling him to bring the injured boy into the house. In this way, Hippias himself might decide on the matter.

Hippias, tyrant of Athens, coming forward in person, preferred to be courteous. He did not care about the lives of a few poor Athenians, foreign exiles, petty traders, sailors, or criminals. In fact, if his bowmen had slaughtered one or two of the rabble, it would have been salutary. But respectable citizens made dangerous martyrs. Hippias was a pale, tall man with eyes of faded blue and hair and beard of indeterminate color, once brown, now not quite gray. But he had the politician's trick of remembering faces, so that he recognized Euphorion at once and could chat with him of his olive groves and neighbors. He could also smile presentably with his lips while polite things were said, press wine on Euphorion, listen to his story, send for his own doctor, and be busy all the while making up his mind. Euphorion was of a class he feared, too numerous to be exiled or put out of the way, too independent to make good subjects. Euphorion might be flattered for the moment into a semblance of good humor, but his misadventure would be reflected in ill-will throughout Eleusis.

"Not much harm done to this boy," Hippias said lightly when the child opened his eyes and tried to sit up. "All boys are tough. My young Pisistratos took such a knock on the head from a stone that he was half out of his senses, but tomorrow he will be none the worse." He shook his head, conveying a half apology for his grandson as well as a suggestion that the damage had not all been on one side. "I have sent to tell my cousin Leucippe that her son is safe, though I will not let him go home until he is recovered. In the meantime, I must offer you the thanks which female shyness will not allow Leucippe to tender in person."

His voice flowed smoothly on, giving him time for reflection. Miltiades could be useful to him at the entrance to the Black Sea, for which reason he had sent him off in a warship with all speed. Yes, the tyrant of the Chersonese could be useful if he would; but there was the matter of Cimon's death between them, never mentioned, never forgotten. What would Miltiades do when he sat securely on a throne of his own, rich in plunder and tolls, a long way off from Athens? Which way would he turn?

This Euphorion was a hard man to charm, and it must not appear that the tyrant stooped to ask his favor. Yet Hippias was aware he did stoop and that his tyranny had descended a long way since the days when his enemies were mighty men of the caliber of Cimon. All the more did he have need of Miltiades to protect Athenian trade. If he lost that and hard times came, it would not be easy to keep himself the master of turbulent Athens.

"My cousin's child is as dear to me as my own," he told Euphorion. It had not hitherto occurred to him, fool that he had been, to give thought to Leucippe. She was only a woman. If she had had the sense to cross to Euboea, as she might have done from Marathon, she could have joined her husband when she pleased. Luckily she had brought her son to Athens, a child of promise if half Euphorion said was true, a handsome boy. Miltiades would do much for such a son. "As dear as my own," he repeated. "I will look after him instead of his father, I promise you. Zeus be my witness."

"My father," muttered the boy, confused. "I must go to my father."

"That must wait until Miltiades's affairs are settled," Hippias smiled.

The Beach at Marathon

THE TOWN of Marathon was a group of houses huddled together for sociability's sake and belonging to those who farmed the plain. These were for the most part well-to-do, since plains and fertile lands were rare in Attica. For this reason, Marathon boasted an exercise ground where children and adults would come to practice at slack times of year, while slaves did most of the field work. Indeed, athletic distinction was a matter of great local pride. Now that Cimon and his fabulous mares were dead, the hero of the place was Aristias, an old Olympic victor who lived off his reputation, condescending to act as coach to young men who showed promise.

It was a gorgeous day, exceptional even in the golden months of an Attic summer. The sun had not yet dried everything out, so that flowers still dotted the plain, which sloped gently from the foothills of jagged Pentelicos to the blue sea. In the clear distance across the narrow strait, the line of Euboea framed the horizon. Bees buzzed past. A lark was singing. Scents of flowers mingled with the dust and smells of well-oiled bodies.

Aristias had swooped on a group of boys who seemed to be arguing instead of exercising as they should.

"Now then, come on there, you! Line up for a foot race!"

He was well aware, though he gave no sign, that his presence would lend any race terrific importance. He did not usually notice boys beyond tossing out a sentence which anyone who was coaching them could pass on. It flattered him to hear Metiochos, son of Miltiades, say, "All right, you'll do it if I win . . ." and see Conon and the others nod. That was competitive spirit! Boys ought to make wagers, and he did not trouble his head about what they were plotting. Let their tutors see to that!

He knew them all well except Metiochos, who was being brought up in Athens, for his education's sake, they said. Miltiades and his father Cimon before him had learned their Homer and studied their music at Marathon. This apparently was not good enough for the son of the tyrant of the Chersonese. Even when they brought the boy down here to acquaint him with the estate he doubtless despised, he had soldiers in attendance. Such nonsense! Two of Hippias's barbarians were actually lounging behind the boys' tutors, who sat keeping close watch on their young charges' behavior.

Aristias would not look at Metiochos; and he put him at the far end of the row, admittedly the worst place for a start. No doubt the boy had coaching from Olympic victors every day and thought nothing of it. He turned to fuss over the others, while young Diomilos muttered out of the corner of his mouth, "Aristias will clear his throat before he gives the word. Count ten when you hear him, and leap immediately. Everyone does it."

Metiochos nodded gratefully. It was possible that Diomilos was trying to disqualify him and get him a beating for starting too early across the line which Aristias was drawing in the sand with his long stick. But he had to take that risk. Besides, he thought Diomilos was jealous of Conon.

His scheme for running away to join his father depended on the help of these boys. It had been easy to impress them with his town polish, his horses, and his chatter of great men. But they would not take any risks unless he could show them that he really was better than they. For one thing, they did not quite trust him yet. Conon was distant kin to a noble family which Hippias had sent into exile. Metiochos had reminded Conon he had less reason to hate the tyrant of Athens than Miltiades did. Conon shook his head, unconvinced.

"Miltiades is a tyrant. They are all the same."

"No, it's different up there," retorted Metiochos hotly, "with barbarian tribes pushing down to the sea and the Persian Empire across the narrow strait in Asia. They have to have a leader."

Conon still looked doubtful, but Aristias had swooped upon them to start the foot race, and the argument had dropped. Metiochos had seen a chance to prove himself and had challenged them all. But Conon was half a head taller and a year older. Callias, too, was light on his feet.

With a tightness in his chest, Metiochos accepted the risk of public shame and public beating to be sure he got away first. Let others count to ten! He heard the cough and made his spring at eight. He was almost certain that his foot had been over the line when the signal was given, but he ran as though for his life.

He won very easily, which he had not expected. Aristias came stalking after them and frowning, the long stick twirling in his hand. It was bitter for Metiochos to know that he would have won anyway and that a moment's panic might have thrown his victory away. He had no one to blame but himself if he were disqualified.

He faced Aristias, who came right up to him scowling. There was an awful silence. "When you run at Olympia," Aristias growled at last, "*if* you run at Olympia, don't try that trick. You were lucky by half a finger's breadth, or I'd take your hide off." He paused impressively. "You'll do for the boys' race at the festival. I'll see to it."

Conon audibly gasped. The rest seemed to freeze up. Metiochos had a mad desire to giggle because all the boys knew that he would never run. But he wanted to cry at the same time because the compliment was the greatest ever paid him. To run in the boys' race! To be numbered among the champions of the future! He desired it so intensely that tears of regret actually pricked his eyes as he blushed and mumbled with a modesty Aristias had not expected of him. Aristias felt his heart warm toward the boy.

"That's settled, then," he said. "You are better than your father." He pulled himself up short. It was fatally easy to give a boy a swelled head. "But then your father had more competition." His eye raked the others, who hung their heads politely. "In my day we would have been ashamed to be out of breath after so little effort. You're all soft!"

He stalked away while they watched, hardly daring to move.

"You'll have to stay now," urged Callias in a whisper. "What wouldn't I give to run in the boys' race?" he sighed with envy.

Metiochos had got over his tears. He looked out to sea and across to Euboea. "No," he informed them curtly. "I won't stay. Not even to run."

They all protested at that, and it was hard to satisfy them because he himself scarcely knew why he must go. He felt no childish desire to run away. He was miserable at the loss of his friends, his dog, his riding horses. As a cousin of Hippias and high in favor, he had Athens at his feet. He could run in the foot race. Later on, he could dance in a chorus, ride in procession at the great Pana-

thenaea, train for Olympia. There was nowhere for enjoying life like Athens when you were a young man.

If he complained about being watched, the boys would
not be impressed. Their own tutors slept with them, attended them every waking minute. No boy was ever left
alone. In fact, they all had guards of a sort and thought
very little of those of Hippias.

If he were to tell them the truth, it would be that Leucippe, growing sallower and more horse-faced every year,
unceasingly blamed him for the watch kept on them both.
As spring followed spring, ships came regularly home past
the Chersonese with Black Sea grain; and messages from
Miltiades came in them. Hippias would answer with excuses. Leucippe, shedding tears, could hardly see her son
without complaining that she was detained on his account.
Her father, too, who made his home with them to oversee
her house, was a sour old man who did not make much
effort to conceal his dislike of the task and his reluctance
to let his own son take charge of his family acres. Metiochos must go because he was not wanted. This, however,
he could not explain to those who admired him because
they thought his life was full of glamor.

"It's such an adventure!" he said, aglow with the excitement of the unknown. What if his father was little in
his memory but a bright figure galloping away in a cloud
of dust? Miltiades was still a warrior chief, a naval captain perched precariously in a corner of the world where
strange things happened. There was much for his heir to
learn which could not be taught him in Athens.

He could see the others did envy him. Not one of them

expected to lounge around Marathon all his days, as Aristias did. Besides, school was so dull and the supervision they lived under was so oppressive that they had to break out from time to time. And they were eager to thwart the tyrant's plans if they could safely do it.

"You wagered with me," he urged. "If I won, you were to help me. Or are you afraid?"

"I'll do it," Conon said. He looked at the others, and they nodded at once. They had been waiting for him. "We'll all do it."

Metiochos glanced cautiously around. The waiting tutors were letting them scrape off dust and perspiration before they collected their charges to go home. There was still a minute or two which was worth using. He lowered his voice.

"In ten days' time when the moon sets very early so that it will be dark, meet me by the sacred olive which stands near the boundary stone of Hermias. And say nothing . . ."

The slave Andrios, who was the boy's tutor now, blinked wearily. He was getting old and usually found himself nodding before the long afternoon was over. A meal would revive him, but soon after sunset Andrios was always snoring in the little, windowless room he shared with his young master.

The house of Miltiades, for all his wealth, was scarcely bigger or better than those of his neighbors. It was built of stone with floors of trodden earth. The rooms of the men, both slave and free, opened out of the great court.

Beyond it, the women had a court of their own, which was private from strangers. Outside was a farm-and-stable-yard where some of the servants slept near the horses, while a watchdog chained at the gate gave warning of strangers. In this way old Cimon had lived, and his father before him, and generations before that. They spent their waking hours out of doors and would have thought it shameful to lounge at home or to furbish up a place used for eating and sleeping.

In his small dark room with Andrios beside him, Metiochos waited for the moon to go down. There were no murmurs from the great court. The servants worked hard and rose up early. They were usually ready for their pallets of straw but there was no knowing whether one of them might not be restless tonight. The guards of Hippias who watched over the boy, for his protection it was pretended, camped in the courtyard.

Metiochos listened anxiously to all the familiar noises. An owl cried and was answered. There were mysterious scufflings on the roof. Wind sighed gently through the great oak which shaded the yard. Somebody muttered, perhaps in his sleep, but who knew? His grandfather was making a dry coughing sound. He might be wakeful.

In any case, it was time to move. He dared not keep the others waiting. In the nighttime, evil spirits were abroad. These boys might see something which frightened them back to their beds. They might be glad to get out of helping him on the pretext that he had not come.

He sat up gently, hearing the leather straps which supported his mattress creak as he moved. There was a break in the rhythm of Andrios's breathing, and he froze. Presently he dared to put a foot down, then another. In careful stages, he shifted his weight off the bed and stood up. Nothing happened. Quietly he lifted his tunic from its peg and slid it on. His cloak, too. If he were noticed crossing the court, a cloak would look odd; but he would need it later against the night air. After a moment of hesitation, he put it on. That capacity which he possessed for taking chances informed him that anyone he met would be too sleepy to trouble himself about what Metiochos was wearing.

Sliding to the door, he peered into the courtyard. A myriad stars were out but, shadowed by four walls, the place was dark. There were benches in it, a water jar, a brazier on which they had mulled wine for the old man before he retired. Here and there stood light tables. A basket or two had been brought in for repair, and perhaps other objects. He started across, trying to remember where movable things had lately been put. He was nearly over when he stubbed his toe on something hard. It shifted, and a jar fell with a little clatter.

"Who's that?" It was his grandfather calling. "Who's out there?"

"Metiochos." He advanced swiftly into the old man's doorway, keeping his voice low. "Metiochos. Just going outside." He meant, to urinate. Manners in the country were informal.

"Ugh! Ugh!" the old man coughed. "Wake me Lydios and have him heat me a honey drink for my cough. Ugh! Ugh! You drink too much water when you come in from the exercise ground. It's not good for your stomach."

"I'll get Lydios." He faded away from the doorway, not too quickly, lest the old man call after him and wake half the house.

Lydios was used to being aroused in the night. He said the drink was ready and that the ashes in the brazier were keeping it warm. Glaucos, who shared a room with him, woke up to curse him for making a noise, thrashed about a little, and seemed to be dropping off. Metiochos wondered whether the bustle had woken Andrios, but he dared not go back to look. If Andrios realized that his charge was out of his bed, he would certainly be up to find out why. Any minute, Lydios might get curious, too. He had better go out.

He went quickly into the court and crossed to the gateway. No one here noticed him. The horses were quiet in their stables. Only the watchdog got up, rattling its chain. He had known that it would do so, and he went across to fondle its ears. It thumped with its tail in the narrow space, beating the wall with a series of dull thuds. He left it and put up both hands to wrestle with the bolt.

Luckily this was only a bar which dropped into a socket on either side of the gate. It was easily lifted and made no sound coming out. He put it carefully beside him on the ground, lest he knock it over. The hinges of the gate were quite another thing. Made of heavy leather, they were bound to creak at the slightest move. All he could do was hold his breath and pull the gate towards him slowly, his heart in his mouth.

Behind him in the stables, someone called out.

He stood perfectly still with both his hands on the door. The man who had heard the sound might still be uncertain what had waked him. The dog was silent. Minutes slid away, seeming like hours. He wondered if Lydios would notice that he had not come back or would go into his room, waking Andrios up, to see if he was there.

At last he dared to move again. The door sounded as though it were crying aloud, such a squeak it gave! This time, no one seemed to hear. The gate was wide enough open for him to wriggle through. He dared not shut it again behind him and hoped that the breeze would not set it swinging.

Standing in the trodden space outside the gate, he thought for a second on all he was leaving behind. His heart was sore. But even as regret tugged at him, new tasks clamored for his attention. He must find his comrades, hurry them across country in the dark to the sea. He must find the boat. It was because of the boat that he had needed help. Alone, he could not have launched it, hoisted the sail, or even set up the steering oar.

The boats that drew up on Marathon beach were of no great size. Athenian trade went in or out of the docks at Phaleron, which served Athens. But there was some direct commerce from Marathon with Euboea. To be sure, the island grew the same products, but there was exchange. Travelers, too, went back and forth. Naturally because there were boats, there was also fishing. In general, however, there was not much living in a boat. There was no community down on the shore and no dock built there. No long voyages were made. A few of the farmers owned part-shares in a boat, captained by one of themselves and manned by slave-oarsmen, who also worked on the land in busy seasons. These went out early and came back in time to walk home in the cool of the evening beside a donkey with panniers carrying their catch.

Miltiades had owned one of these boats, which did his errands. Demetrios, who captained it, was a sly, plausible man, fit for intrigues if there was profit in them, but preferring small things to great. Leucippe, desperate in her need, had spoken with him, almost believing that she, who had never been out of her house without an escort, dared entrust herself to a strange man for a journey clear across the Aegean Sea. She had been too timid, however, to be frank. Demetrios had not taken her hints, having no fancy to brave the wrath of Hippias. Afterwards, Leucippe in her endless complaints used to claim that he had warned their guards. Since then, at all events, he had treated the vessel as his private property, selling his catch in the open market and retaining the money which he earned by traffic with Euboea.

Conon was leading the way down to the beach. The plain was cultivated, but there were trees and tangled thickets to be skirted as well as vines and olives. At the north end of the beach in front of the harbor lay a marsh. It was not possible to hurry across such ground without making noise; and though their families were all at Marathon in bed, there might be strange things listening. Indeed, the night seemed full of sounds. Trees rustled mysteriously. Owls cried in the distance. The scream of a rabbit rent the air. Even the breakers seemed to be concealing movements on the beach.

"What's that?" Conon stood still to listen.

"A dog howling."

"That's no dog," Metiochos contradicted. "That's a horse neighing, and not far off either. Listen!"

The sound stopped.

Callias shivered. "People say that horses race the plain at night and men in armor ride them. Not everyone sees them, but those who do are fated . . ."

"I saw nothing at all," replied Meticohos quickly.

"But you heard them. Conon did, too."

"Then the ill luck is not yours." He spoke sharply, anxious to head off panic, though frightened lest unseen spirits take him at his word. "Where is this boat, Conon? Surely we should be near it."

Conon halted in his turn. "It isn't here."

Metiochos shook his arm. "You saw Demetrios come home tonight. We all saw him. We must have passed it."

"No," Callias said with authority. "I counted the others; and besides, I know them well. It isn't here."

"Then it must be down on the south shore." Metiochos was impatient. "What possessed Demetrios to draw it up there tonight of all nights?"

"I know what possessed him," Callias whispered. "It's on the south shore that shadows move on the beach — a great press of men. If you see them . . ."

"I tell you, I saw nothing," said Metiochos in a fierce

whisper. "Neither horses, nor riders, nor men on the beach. Are you frightened?"

"Yes, of course."

"Then I will lead the way, and you follow." He started down the beach. After a moment, they stumbled after him, all bunched together.

The boat lay on the south shore, which was perfectly quiet and no more shadowy than the harbor had been. They grouped about it, putting their shoulders against its side, and heaved. It did not move.

"All together and she'll come. Wait for the word, and . . . heave!" She moved about a foot with a grating sound.

"Heave!" Metiochos was shouting at them in a hoarse whisper. Over the sound of their slipping feet and the grating of the keel, his word came back to him, echoed perhaps, and yet from where? "Heave! Heave!"

The others did not seem to hear. The keel was nearing the water; and in another minute she would be afloat. But there really were movements in the shadows on the beach, whispers of sound so faint that he could not be certain of them. It was rather that the gasps and grunts of the boys were too loud, the sliding of the keel in the pebbly sand was audible for a second or so after the boat had ceased to move. In fact, these noises were being used to cover others. He was so sure of it that his voice seemed to choke in his throat as he tried to shout, "Heave!"

At last she slid away with a rush. Metiochos got wet to the waist wading out to catch a rope. He would be cold later, but did not care much now. He scrambled aboard, the rest behind him. Conon groped for the anchor stone and flung it out.

"Better set the steering oar first." They lifted the clumsy thing and hung it in its socket to trail astern. They untied the halyards, hauled up the heavy sail, and left it flapping. "You tie it here!" Conon showed Metiochos what to do. "If you want to, you may lash the steering oar as well. You can't miss Euboea."

"Visit me in the Chersonese," Metioches told them. "We owe you a great debt, my father and I. Meanwhile, you had better get back before you are missed, so that nobody can be blamed for this night's work."

Conon laughed. "It is a pity. I should dearly like to boast of it. As for Callias, he is longing to tell everyone that there is nothing in the story of a ghostly landing on Marathon beach at midnight."

"Not a landing!" Metiochos answered almost absently as he listened for the echo. "No, not a landing! Those ghosts were in a mad panic to get away. Didn't you feel them?"

Eretria

On the morning of the second day, Metiochos knocked on the door of Tisander, who was his father's cousin and one of the wealthiest of the ruling nobles of Eretria. Now Eretria was one of the two chief territories of Euboea.

The porter who opened the door sniffed dubiously. Metiochos was filthy, flea-bitten, and stank of cheese. He had spent the night with a peasant and had staggered into town with him, loaded with a basket of his evil smelling wares.

"Go away!" said the porter, who was a man of few words. He banged the door.

Metiochos picked up a stone and hammered noisily. Presently the door shot open again, and the porter grabbed him. "You dirty guttersnipe, you! Get out!" He tried to cuff him.

"I am your master's cousin," cried the boy wriggling. "His cousin. I . . ."

"Get out!"

But when the door was shut again and the boy did not go, but stood crying that he was the master's cousin and beating upon it, the porter scratched a slow head. People had all sorts of cousins. If the master had been in, he would never have dared disturb his leisure with this one. But since he was out . . .

At this point in his reasoning, the porter went to fetch the master's confidential servant, who made him open the door to the boy at once. Lykos listened to the child's account of his adventures and sent for Tisander. He did not offer any refreshment, perceiving that the boy's appearance was part of the strangeness of the affair and that Tisander would want to inspect him. Besides, though he inclined to the view that there must be something behind the story, he did not believe what he had been told. For such an escape, this child was simply too young.

Tisander, when he came in, said hardly a word. He was a slender man with a long, thin face and bony fingers which he rubbed together while he took time to consider. Eventually he said, politely enough, that his young cousin must take a bath and some refreshment. No need to talk of further plans till later. But when attendants had taken the boy away, he turned to his servant, with whom he was on intimate terms.

"Well, Lykos?"

Lykos, who looked like an intelligent rat, shook his head. "I think not."

Tisander drummed his fingers on the carved arm of his chair. "I think not, too. The thing's impossible. To escape from Hippias at twelve years old, or is he thirteen? Miltiades's people would have smuggled him out long ago if it had been easy."

"He has a look of Miltiades," Lykos said. "Even if this story is the purest fantasy, he may be the right boy."

"Awkward."

"Very awkward, sir. Whatever will you tell him?"

Tisander made no answer to that beyond complaining that a month ago he would have sent the boy on to his cousin, whereas now he did not know what to do. Miltiades might not thank him for interfering.

Lykos reminded him that since Miltiades's ship was still in port, there might be someone on it who really knew his son. Besides, the messenger Miltiades had sent might bear instructions about what was to be done with the boy in this new situation.

Tisander agreed, relieved to have put off deciding anything. A few hours later when he sent for Metiochos, he had with him a lean, brown man in a coarse brown cloak who simply nodded.

"That's the one."

Tisander hardly knew how to treat the boy if all he heard about him were true. He drew out a stool, almost as though he had been a man and an equal. "Sit down beside me. Do you remember Cleon, who is now one of your father's ship captains?"

The boy stared inquiringly at Cleon for a moment, then shook his head. "I do not think I ever saw him."

Cleon laughed. "We met in Athens. You were younger, but you were running away then, too."

This brought Metiochos to his feet with snap of the fingers. "Oh yes, I remember! The man with the big . . . well, with the big nose! You boxed my ears."

Cleon made a swing in the air. "I might do it again if your tongue is so free. Big nose indeed! Sit down and tell me how you got here."

The boy began shyly enough, but Cleon's questions forced out facts. He had not dared ask any man to help him escape. The tyrant Hippias was terrible these days when people defied him. He had thought of the boat by himself, and also of the boys, who would not be suspected. Oh, he had planned it all for more than a year.

It was matter-of-fact and rang true. Cleon kept stealing sideways glances at Tisander as if to say, "What did I tell you about this boy?"

There was a difficult silence when the tale was ended. Tisander still rubbed the tips of his fingers together, turning them over at intervals to inspect them. Thoughtfully he bit his lip. The boy looked inquiringly at him, glanced back at Cleon, blinked, and fidgeted. He was well enough brought up to know he must not put questions to grown men, but his impatience had been suppressed for so long that he could not quite control it. "Well," he said finally in an uncertain voice, "Here I am!"

Tisander frowned, displeased. "Cleon has errands on your father's behalf and must discharge them before he sails for home. No need to hasten him."

The boy blushed at the reproof. He swallowed anxiously. His large, dark eyes looked inquiringly for a moment at Tisander. Then, fearing to give further offence, they slid off him and began to roam about the room as though their purpose had been to make an inventory of its contents.

Abruptly Tisander got up. "I have a treasure to show you." He walked over to a small chest beautifully inlaid with ivory which sat on his painted floor between a graceful table and a much heavier chest with a great lock. Grunting a little, Tisander lifted the box to the table and threw back the lid.

Metiochos, peering politely, felt disappointment. It was only a book box, partitioned into squares for the safe keeping of manuscript rolls. The tyrant Hippias had such a thing, and his household had listened at various times to readings from it. Metiochos had learned by heart a few of the war songs, which he privately thought were less old-fashioned than Homer.

Tisander ignored the parchment rolls and lifted out a thin sheet of copper which he took pains to smooth flat with careful fingers. "Have you ever seen a map like this? It is a picture of the shape of the world; and it was drawn by Hecataeus, who has written describing the world, both Europe and Asia."

He began to point out places to the boy, explaining that here was Athens, here Eretria, and how a day's journey on such a picture as this was too small to be seen. "Why, this is the whole Aegean Sea as it might look to a god a long way off, so tiny that you can cover it with your hand."

"And here," added Cleon, craning over his shoulder, "is the dominion of the Great King, Darius the Persian."

Tisander looked up and caught Cleon's eye. He nodded approval even as his finger moved across the map. "Yes, indeed! Here lies the Great King, and here, and here . . . Here is Egypt, where he has a war fleet of at least two hundred ships which are always ready. Here is Phoenicia, where he has as many more. In Asia Minor, the Greek cities of the coast hold their fleets at his service. Far inland lies Susa, his capital city, where he commands a guard of ten thousand soldiers. Their spears are butted with silver or gold, and they are known as the Immortals because when any man dies another is ready to step into his place. And the Great King has many thousand other warriors in Media, Bactria, Cappadocia, Lydia —in all the countries of the East, which stretch to the edge of the world. None can number the King's armies."

This time it was Cleon's turn to nod. The conversation

seemed to be directed at the boy, and yet the grown
men passed it back and forth over his head as though they
were playing a kind of ball between themselves which he
was not supposed to notice.

Metiochos had bent over the map and was trying to understand it. "Persia! That must be a long way off."

Tisander caught Cleon's eye again. "A long way indeed!
It is a three months' journey from the King's capital at
Susa to the coast near the Chersonese. And Susa is only
the center of the King's dominions."

"The Chersonese!" The boy peered at the map, more
interested in his father's territory than in all the lands of
Darius the Persian. He looked eagerly at the place where
Tisander's finger lay and wished he were in it. Like Attica, the Chersonese was very small on the map, a mere
line representing a jagged peninsula stretched out along
the narrow strait which divided Asia from Europe.
Metiochos was glad of its size. How could a man really
care about a country which he could not ride across in a
day or two?

"The Chersonese!" echoed Tisander gently. "Here sits
your father, and here commences the land of Darius the
Persian. There is only the strait between them, at its nar-
rowest part no more than a mile. There are rivers wider."

"But . . . but . . ." Metiochos's finger traced clum-
sily the three months' journey between the coast and
Susa. That incredible distance did away with a vague
alarm.

"Let me ask you," Tisander inquired in the same measured tone, still directing his words above the boy's bent head, "How many warships has your father?"

The boy did not know. He looked up at Cleon.

"Five."

"And how many hundreds has the Great King? They may be far away, but ships can move. Have you seen ships come into Phaleron docks with cargoes from Egypt?"

Speechlessly the boy nodded.

"Fleets move and armies move," agreed Cleon, bending down to emphasize his words by tracing movements on the map with his forefinger. Tisander still watched him and not the child.

"Yet the movements of such forces take time," he reminded Cleon, taking up his part in a lesson which clearly had a goal which both were aware of, though they hung back from speaking plainly to the boy.

"Besides, King Darius may sometimes need his armies elsewhere," Cleon said.

"Yet tell me, Metiochos," Tisander again took his turn. "If you were your father and across the straits lay such a king who could swallow you when he pleased, what would you do?"

Metiochos had thought of this already, and his tongue tripped over itself trying to explain how many Greek cities lay all along that coast, rich in ships and men.

"Most of the tyrants of the Hellespont," put in Cleon, frowning darkly, "would as soon submit to the Great King and pay him tribute. They think he will uphold them in their positions. There is hardly a city in those parts whose people do not wish to get rid of their tyrant."

"Like Athens," Tisander agreed.

"Yes, like Athens. Only Miltiades, whose people really need him, desires freedom."

By now the argument of the two men was going so briskly that they did not so much as glance down at the boy to discover that he had gone first white, then red, and was blinking back tears. It had occurred to Metiochos that his father must be dead and the barbarian already in the Chersonese. For there was something, he understood very well, which they wanted to tell him.

"All the same, the boy is in the right," Tisander continued smoothly. "Miltiades needs to make allies. How else can he survive?"

"He cannot live otherwise," agreed Cleon, receiving this remark and tossing it back.

"Now Thrace . . ." Tisander gave a pause after the name as though at last he had come in sight of something which he had been making for. "Thrace stretches inland . . ."

The boy was not listening any longer. He put his face into his hands and burst into loud sobs. Tisander patted his shoulder in dismay, inquiring whatever the matter could be. This merely served to make his crying worse.

Tisander's fingers interlaced themselves again in agitation. He called all the gods to witness he had done nothing, said nothing, and told Metiochos nothing at all.

"That's the trouble." Cleon merely looked grim. "Give the boy a drink."

Tisander mixed a cup of wine and water from vessels set ready near the door. In his hurry he spilled it and had to pour again. When he took it over to Metiochos, the boy would not take his hands from his face. He was crouched in a corner, crying with a tempestuous passion which seemed uncontrollable.

"The boy is only tired." Lykos, who always knew when he was wanted, poked his sharp nose through the doorway. Firmly he walked across to Metiochos and took him by the arm. "You will feel better soon when you have rested. Can you walk with me, or shall I have you carried?"

His tone, though not unkind, was matter-of-fact. It worked wonders. The boy still gulped convulsively, but he allowed himself to be helped to his feet and led out of the room.

Tisander, whose cup was still in his hand, drained it off, forgetting in his agitation the duties of a host. He sank into his chair with a sigh, caught up the edge of his cloak, and wiped his forehead. "Lykos will tell him. Lykos does everything. I can't."

"But what shall I do with him when he knows?" Cleon demanded. "Do I take him with me or send him back? You must make up your mind."

Tisander was playing with his fingers again. Receiving no inspiration from this source, he stared blankly at Cleon, who would not meet his gaze but shrugged his shoulders as though throwing responsibility off. Tisander sighed heavily once more.

"That letter you carry," he said at last. "It must say something about the boy. Do you know what is in it?"

Cleon fumbled under his cloak. Under the girdle of his

tunic he was carrying a letter which consisted of a pair of wooden tablets fastened together with a thread and sealed with wax, a little melted by now with the heat of his body. He took it in his hand to show Tisander that the seal, though damaged, was recognizable as the chariot and horses which Miltiades still used in memory of his brother.

"He made no secret of its contents. Thus it says: 'I have married the daughter of the King of Thrace. Therefore let Leucippe, daughter of Ariphron, go home to her father's house, taking her dowry and those things which are properly hers in case of divorce.' "

Tisander shook his head in despair. There were decencies which ought to have been observed in this matter. Why be so blunt? Why celebrate the marriage first? Why not mention the boy? He said something of this sort to Cleon, who merely pointed out that the king's daughter had read the letter. She had a new Greek name, Hegesiphyle, or Princess. In her own tongue she was called something else which Miltiades had translated for common use into Melissa. He was in love.

Tisander groaned aloud. Had it not been for the arrival of Metiochos, he would have approved of this match. The alliance was certainly a prudent one. What use was Leucippe to a man in the Chersonese? And how much longer must Miltiades dance at Hippias's bidding because of his son? They all knew that Hippias had a brother who reigned as tyrant across the straits, paying tribute to the Great King of Persia. Thus if only to regain his freedom of action, Miltiades should have more sons. Now he would do so, and the future tyrant of the Chersonese would be a child of this Princess. Her father, King Oloros of Thrace, would see to that.

He fingered his beard, which was thin and straggled a little. That letter had been dictated by a jealous woman! Miltiades was in love! What weakness in a man, especially in a husband! She had not even let him mention his son.

Cleon broke in on his thoughts impatiently. "Well, shall I take the boy with me, or will you send him back to his mother? For my part, if I found I had such a son, I would not cast him off."

The statement was carelessly made, but it impressed Tisander. He was a cultured man, more used to intrigue than he was to action. Cleon, who had been everywhere and carried mysterious scars from a dozen remote quarters of the world, was a puzzle to him. But he had observed that if he ever agreed with such a man, they were probably right.

"Take him with you," Tisander ordered, provoked into a decision which he had not weighed and balanced with delicate care. "Let Miltiades judge the boy for himself." He bit at his forefinger as doubt nagged him. Melissa! A pet name for a jealous woman! "What happens thereafter may rest on the lap of the gods, not on mine. Let them see to the future."

Earth and Water

At the season of the year when spring moved into summer, snows had melted on the mountains of Thrace. Bogs were drying. Streams no longer ran in spate. At such a time it soon became the custom for Miltiades and Melissa with their little girl and most of their attendants to visit Oloros, king of Thrace. His Thracian alliance had freed Miltiades from frontier perils. For many years he had not lain down on his bed without hanging his sword on a convenient peg beside it. Now shepherds and goatherds in the sandy scrub were safe from casual raiding. The smaller areas where vines and grain and olives grew could now be harvested without disturbance. Miltiades was free to look up and down the strait, where his five little cities were a principality to be reckoned with, as long as one did not stare at Asia or calculate the power of the Persian king.

Miltiades, still in the prime of life, was too large a personality to live content in the shadow of a great empire. He aspired to rule the North Aegean and its islands, which might, given luck and leadership, hold off the Persians. Better far for the Greek cities that they unite under their own kin than that they fall subject to the barbarian one by one. Such were their jealousies, however, that the ambition of one was resented by all. Miltiades was powerless without the backing of Oloros; but the Thracian was a wily man who took time to think over where his best interests lay. Besides, he was an inland monarch and suspicious of naval adventures. Thus the visit that Miltiades annually made was only on the surface a holiday to him. So far King Oloros had neither refused nor granted his requests. Presently without some Thracian help the North Aegean and the Chersonese itself would fall to the Persian.

Melissa, clad in barbarian costume for the occasion, did not concern herself with political issues. She would be in wild spirits. The Princess was a big girl with a brown complexion and a mass of auburn hair which she knotted behind. Strands of this escaped around her face in the wind, for she would not wear hat or scarf upon these journeys. Like the men, she rode donkeyback, since much of the terrain was rough for horses. Melissa's donkey was always trotting forward up the line or straying from the path so that Melissa could catch sight of a bird, pick a flower, or call to a shepherd. Melissa's voice, which was full and rich, was always rising in song, sometimes in a war chant which the men hummed to themselves, and at other moments in wild barbarian strains. Melissa's eyes, which were almost golden in color, twinkled at the men of the escort with a frankness which greatly embarrassed them. Even in the Chersonese, Melissa was not Greek enough to keep out of sight. On holiday, she behaved with a freedom which was shocking.

In the first year after his coming, Metiochos was included in this party. In secret, Miltiades was afraid lest the boy's absence offend the Thracian, who must have heard of his coming. Melissa's own welcome to her husband's son had been constrained. She had not a son of her own as yet, but she fully expected to bear Miltiades an heir. She was inclined to be jealous. All the same, it was not in her nature to live on open bad terms. Metiochos had an ear for music as keen as her own. He had new songs to teach her. Miltiades, though eager to praise the lad, was quick to point out that there were other inheritances than the Chersonese, in Athens, for instance, or perhaps one of the islands.

Handled in such a way, Metiochos's coming had caused no quarrels in Miltiades's household. He himself was proud of the boy, while for Melissa's sake he was happy that she should adopt him almost as a playmate. She would not have charmed Miltiades so much if she had been blamelessly conventional like poor Leucippe. Yet he knew that Melissa went too far in appearing among men. He was glad when her attention was distracted from public affairs by the boy in her household.

Looking back on that fair summer journey later, the boy thought of it as a golden time. He and Melissa were laughing, playing tricks on each other like a pair of colts loose in the springtime. They would sing to the lark in the clear blue sky; and the bird, rising higher, would answer them back with a cascade of notes. They would splash each other when they forded a stream. When they camped beside one, they would wade in the pools or count the fish, which Melissa was expert in catching when she pleased to take the trouble. She would teach him barbarian words or get him to tell her the Greek names for the stars while their tents were being pitched. He would lie in wait for her every morning, "like a dog," Miltiades said, but he smiled as he said it. Before them would be the whole long day full of innocent pleasure.

All changed abruptly when they arrived. Melissa vanished into the midst of a crowd of chattering brothers and sisters whose comments and laughter Metiochos could not understand. King Oloros, who spoke Greek, was heavily courteous to him. Indeed, his labored welcome was embarrassing. Metiochos hung his head and blushed. Behind him, Miltiades lowered black brows in a frown. But King Oloros went on with his smooth periods notwithstanding.

King Oloros was a tall, heavy-featured man with hair of a dark red. Low-voiced and quiet of manner, he presented a great contrast to his chattering brood of children. It was notable, however, that at his least gesture servants came running, as though they dared not allow a second's delay. His children perhaps were not afraid of him, and yet they treated him with a respect that almost amounted to awe. In his presence Melissa cast down her eyes and held her tongue in a modest fashion which she never attempted with Miltiades.

Metiochos soon regretted he had come. He was exhausted by the interminable length of a feast in barbarian fashion at long tables in the great hall, with ill-bred dogs snarling over morsels and servants hurrying to fill every cup with wine or beer. Besides, Oloros did not get drunk in a jolly fashion. Wine made him more tedious than ever. Miltiades, whose business it was to be pleased, smiled diplomatically and assented to all the king said. Metiochos, longing for bed, was peering around him to estimate his chances of slipping away when those who sat next him fell suddenly silent. Looking up, he discovered that Oloros was speaking to him again. He was inviting him to use the royal stables.

Really grateful, Metiochos stammered his thanks. In the Chersonese there was hardly anywhere a horse could go, since the peninsula was a tangle of jagged little peaks and stony ravines. Riding, which had been a passion of his, was one thing he missed. Immediately, he made up his mind that King Oloros and his kingdom were not bad.

In the succeeding days, he spent most of his time in the

stable and learned to talk to the grooms in a pidgin mixture of Greek and barbarian words filled out with gestures. Oloros's horses were beautifully trained, even more so than those he had been used to at home. Indeed, Metiochos's only complaint was that he soon discovered the men would only put him up on gentle horses.

"I ride big gray," he demanded.

A shake of the head. "Big gray too savage."

"White-leg then."

"White-leg lame."

"White star, then."

The head groom threw up his hands, but it seemed to Metiochos that he did so with less emphasis.

"I ride well," he insisted, trying again.

"Very well."

"Then I ride White Star."

"Bay horse," suggested the groom hopefully.

Metiochos made a rude noise which disposed of the bay horse and made the groom grin.

"White Star."

After a few days of this sort of badgering, the groom relented to the extent of agreeing that Metiochos might mount White Star inside the paddock, which was a natural exercise ground, bounded by a streamlet, a wood fringed by a tangled thicket, and the stable.

They bridled the horse for him and put on the usual saddle, which was only a rough blanket strapped beneath. When they led him forth, however, displaying his paces, the groom shook his head teasingly.

"White Star too big."

"I ride him," Metiochos insisted. He jumped forward, seized the bridle, and scrambled onto the creature's back. White Star danced a little and, controlled by the bridle, settled into a canter over the meadow.

Metiochos urged him into a gallop. Already from the first movement he had perceived White Star was totally different from the slower horses of the king which he had bestridden. Now he tasted the pleasure he had not experienced since Athens of being one with the creature he rode. A hand on the bridle, the barest touch of a heel was sufficient to guide him.

They went across the meadow like the wind, turned on the bank of the stream, and came back in a canter. The boy was laughing with pure joy, and the bridle was light in his hands. The groom, who had advanced out into the meadow to meet him, put two fingers into his mouth and gave a piercing whistle. White Star went suddenly mad.

He reared up on his hind legs with a loud whinny. The boy, whose knees were not strong enough to keep him from sliding down to the tail, dropped his bridle and clung for dear life to the mane. This saved him for a crowded second or two in which the horse gathered its strength for a leap into the air. An instant later it returned to the ground on all four feet with a bone-breaking crash which jarred every tooth in its rider's head and must have dislodged him, save by the chance that he fell back across the creature's body. Without a pause White Star tucked his head down and kicked out with his heels. This was too much for Metiochos. He went over White Star's head like a stone from a sling and fell on the ground.

He did not get up, which perhaps was lucky for him, for the horse continued to buck and lash out with his hooves. The stable attendants had gathered in a circle as though they intended to rush in and seize the bridle. No one, however, risked life or limb to do so.

Metiochos's life was probably saved by the action of Cleon, who for reasons of his own was never far from the boy's side that summer. Cleon had not seen the trouble start, but he had heard the whistle and appeared to watch Metiochos fall off. Unable to run to the rescue in time, he picked up a jagged stone and hurled it at the horse.

It hit White Star on the muzzle, cutting the skin and drawing blood. The horse whinnied in a shrill scream and turned away, bucking down the length of the meadow with most of the grooms running after him.

Metiochos was found to have two broken ribs. While these were being bandaged, Cleon sought out Miltiades. It had been no accident, he said. The boy's life had been attempted. Miltiades went to Oloros in glowing indignation.

Oloros was very smooth and unconcerned. His groom, he said, had been pestered by the boy until he determined to teach him a lesson. The stupid slave had not foreseen any danger in his roughness. For this he deserved to be punished and should be so. The groom vanished, and the rumor was that Oloros threw him into his dungeon, which was nothing but a great pit into which the king's jailors dropped down live rats to keep prisoners company.

However this may have been, there was no more riding. Relations with Oloros were strained, and Melissa was no longer gay. The return journey was undertaken as soon as the boy was able to travel. Miltiades looked careworn, and there was no more straying from the path with Melissa. It was known already that she was to have another child, and she rode soberly.

Thus quietly they all came home to settle into their former life. Melissa was soon lighthearted again and teased Metiochos about his riding. But during her pregnancy she did not go out of doors and, perhaps for this reason, had her temperamental humors. It was noticeable, for instance, that if Miltiades paid attention to his son, she flew into a passion or sulked because he was neglecting her. On the whole, things were not as pleasant as they had been, not even when Melissa bore a great, fair son, whom his father named Cimon.

Soon it was summer again and time for another visit to Oloros. Miltiades, it now appeared, would not take Metiochos. He made excuses. His son was nearly fifteen, an awkward age. Miltiades would not accuse his father-in-law, but he did think that the roughness of last year's practical joke had malice behind it. He did not say so to Melissa or even tell her a growing boy ought to spend less time with the women.

"If he were in Athens," he had growled once, observing how Cleon looked gloomily on as Melissa beckoned, "why, then he could ride with the young men and do frontier service. Here I have nowhere to send hm."

He meant out of reach of Melissa, and Cleon understood

him. "Leave him with me this summer to train with your warship crews. I'll make him a man."

"He's young."

"The greater the challenge, and in these times men grow up fast."

In this way the matter was arranged. It is true that Melissa cried out against the plan, but she was too happy to be long out of humor. Her son grew handsomer every day, and she savored the pleasure of displaying him as Miltiades's heir at the court of Oloros. Thus she gave in with a good grace, and she rode away singing.

It happened that this summer was a period of profound peace throughout the Aegean. Most of Cleon's rowers had been trained in previous years, and his ships were in good condition. Nevertheless, the little cities which studded the route to the Black Sea all had their connections with wealthy competitors for the trade. They reflected, often in a violent way, great rivalries elsewhere. Miltiades had learned he must always be ready for trouble by sea as well as by land.

There was plenty to be done even if nothing was urgent. Cleon taught Metiochos the duties of a shipmaster, showed him how to detect a botched repair, what to call for from the storage sheds. He made him plan and direct small naval maneuvers. When the hard work was over, he took him to lounge about the docks or marketplace, listening to sailors from foreign ports swap their stories. Afterwards Cleon would question him on what had been said.

"The Great King is coming to Sardis in person," re-

marked a captain from Miletos, who had put into Sestos
for the night.

The information was buried amid a half-dozen pieces
of news, and Cleon received it with a laugh and an incredu-
lous shrug of the shoulders. All the same, as he pointed out
to Metiochos later, he fastened on the subject.

"When?" he asked in a casual tone.

The captain did not know. Next year perhaps. Cleon
questioned other captains discreetly lest, when they knew
what he was at, they invent answers. He learned nothing.
All they wanted to discuss was a promising quarrel between
Cyme and Phocaea which had been suddenly settled.

"Why did they not fight it out?" said Cleon to the boy.
"On orders from Sardis? This is the third dispute which
has come to nothing. Such peace is unnatural and has
some meaning."

These were worldwide speculations, different from
anything the boy had heard in Athens, even though the
Athenians lived by trade. For the Chersonese looked out
on the world in a startling fashion which made newcomers
catch their breath. Behind it lay the Aegean Sea with
Grecian islands rising out of the water like distant mountains. In front lay the narrow strait, a blue stream in a
valley, with Europe on one side and Asia on the other.
The eastern continent filled the whole horizon from north
of east to furthest southward, where Mount Ida rose into
the sky above the Trojan plain. It reminded Metiochos of
the map Tisander had shown him, on which the whole
Aegean appeared as though seen by a god.

All summer long, brown sails of ships lay like leaves on

the blue strait. So strong did the current set that ships returning homeward to the Aegean sped down the forty-mile strait in a day if the wind were behind them. But a fat cargo boat tacking upstream with men toiling a long day at the oars might take over a week to pass the same small distance.

It was on the painful slowness of this passage that the cities of the Chersonese lived. The towns were scattered up the straits in tiny harbors where weary crews put in at dark. These paid harbor dues, bought victuals, made repairs, sold a little of their cargo, or purchased the hides and lumps of precious metal which came down to the coast from Thrace on the backs of men or donkeys.

Trade was the life of the Chersonese, and trade meant news. Up through the straits ran countless ship routes like lines upon the map, from Athens on the Greek mainland, from Corinth on the Isthmus, from Argos in the Peloponnese, the enemy of Sparta. Ships drew lines from islands, too, like Samos, mistress of the southern sea, whose trading connections also reached south to Egypt. Greek cities of the Asia Minor coast, who were wealthier than any others, sent ships which paid tribute to the Great King's governor in Sardis. These trade lines crossed with other lines drawn into Miletos from Asia Minor and the East, into Samos from Phoenicia, into Corinth from Italian cities and the western sea. The pattern formed a spider web on which any disturbance passed quivering messages through the Chersonese.

An Athenian ship came into Sestos at the narrows in such excitement that it did not wait to come alongside the dock before the captain was on its prow announcing in bull-like tones: "Murder of Hippias's brother at Athene's festival! Widespread conspiracy against the tyrant!"

Sestos, which had the best harbor and stood at the narrows of the strait, was largely an Athenian town. Its male inhabitants were crowding the docks to hear the latest from home. The consequence was a near riot as people pushed forward to get close enough to hear. Expatriates in these parts hated Hippias. Besides, Sigeum, a rival city across the strait, was ruled by his brother. There were wild celebrations in Sestos that night, and hope persuaded the people that Hippias would fall. Next morning a group of elders waited on the palace to suggest Miltiades had better be sent for.

Metiochos received them in the throne room, which was used as court of appeal and council chamber. He was aware that he was only by courtesy consulted, but Cleon had told him he should play for time. Was it prudent to offend the king of Thrace? There was nothing to be done unless Hippias should really fall.

These arguments soon gave Metiochos a reputation for prudence beyond his years. Hippias did not fall. Later ships brought exiles fleeing to their kinsmen in the Chersonese. A purge was raging in Athens which swept away innocent and guilty alike. There was no resistance because the Athenians had been thoroughly disarmed.

The elders at Sestos perceived that they had nearly been rash, and that the boy had restrained them. Their approval began to show itself by entrusting him with duties. Metiochos sat in his father's seat at the midsummer festival which the Sestians celebrated with choral dances. He made a proclamation. He received some ambassadors, whose business was later transacted with the council. In short, he proved a convenient figurehead on occasions when a little extra ceremony was demanded.

In a tumult of pity and dismay over the news at Athens, Sestos paid small attention to a rumor that the Great King was gathering his forces. Only Cleon looked concerned.

"If, as they think, he plans an expedition to the north of the Black Sea, why come to Sardis? Will he collect a fleet to ship through our straits? There is trouble brewing."

Even Metiochos did not pay much heed to these forebodings. His heart was wrung for his own friends in Athens. Besides, there were a thousand new ideas in his mind.

Ideas as well as news passed through the straits. They seemed to be squeezed out of the cities of Greece by internal excitement. Travelers had no notion of keeping knowledge to themselves. They would stop an extra day in Sestos, simply to argue the nature of matter or the origin of the universe. They described with lavish gestures or sketches in the dust great works of engineering. They explained the mathematics of musical harmony or the speculations of Pythagoras about the soul. Metiochos found so much to take in that mutterings of a storm which never broke seemed as distant from him as the changing moods of Melissa.

He was sitting outside a barber shop in a corner of the open marketplace, listening to someone who had seen an eruption of Vesuvius and could tell you that the tale of a giant chained beneath that mountain was all nonsense. The narrator, fending off a number of questions, was thoroughly enjoying his lecture. This made it all the more startling when he opened his mouth, threw out his hand with a dramatic gesture, and seemed to freeze for an instant, speechless. As though pulled by a single string, the listeners turned sharp about to see what had paralyzed him.

Two men were entering the marketplace from the seaward end, an escort of soldiers behind them, and a crowd of citizens pushing at their heels. They were dark men in the prime of life, looking almost unnaturally tall because of their high brimless hats and trailing garments. These last were woven in bands of brilliant color and gleamed with embroidery. Black beards fell on their chests and black hair down the napes of their necks, all carefully curled. They wore big earrings studded with colored stones and rings on their fingers. They carried no weapons, but in their hands they held long staves.

They advanced into the marketplace, looking around without curiosity or haste at the small wooden temple, the new stone one not yet half-finished, the open spaces, the wickerwork market stalls, and the crowd. They moved with a slowness which was almost indolence; and yet there was nothing languid or effeminate about them. Wide sleeves fell back from sunburned wrists, displaying muscles. They held themselves like warriors. Behind them came half a dozen soldiers in leather caps and tunics, wearing loose trousers. These carried spears and had short swords at their sides. Among them walked an elderly man with an iron-gray beard in Grecian costume.

The Sestians milled about these figures in confusion, parting in front of their slow advance until they came to the center of the open space and stopped there. The soldiers divided their ranks, and from between them the little Greek emerged.

He came out a pace in front of his motionless leaders, putting up a hand to ask for silence. There was a hush straightaway. The Sestians were wise enough in world affairs to know what must be coming.

The small Greek lifted up his voice until it rang through the marketplace. "O Sestians, King Darius, the Great King, King of Kings, One King of Many, the Persian, sends envoys to the tyrant of the Chersonese."

A hand fell on Metiochos's shoulder, making him jump. Cleon put down his head to hiss in the boy's ear. "Get up to the palace! Run, do you hear? And scrub that pitch off your arms!"

Metiochos gasped, realizing suddenly that he would have to be concerned in this matter. Here he stood in the gaping crowd, disheveled and grubby, wearing a tunic which had seen duty in the shipyard for many days. He began to worm himself out, panic-stricken lest some officious citizen discover his presence and haul him out as he was to welcome the envoys.

As a matter of fact, it was easily a half hour later before the elders of Sestos had collected and the throne room had been swept out. Miltiades's palace, though larger than the farm at Marathon, was scarcely more luxurious. In the

men's quarters at least, the chief decorations were weapons
on the walls. In his throne room, Miltiades had a carved
chair, beside which stood stools for his council of six elders.
Most of his guards he had taken with him. Those remaining were really household slaves who did the menial
work and looked like brigands when called upon to act as
though they were soldiers.

The elders were only a trifle more imposing. In a town
like Sestos, twenty-five thousand inquisitive people would
not tolerate a man dressing better than his neighbors
merely because he owned a chest full of silver. He had
better put his money into a statue for the marketplace or
fittings for a warship. The elders of Sestos were not stupid
people, but they did not look like an aristocracy.

Metiochos sat perched on the throne with his heart
thumping. His arms were sore from scrubbing off pitch.
His hair was wet from a hasty wash and needed cutting.
Yet the contrast between his smooth young face and the
bearded elders was not without a dignified effect. As they
had explained to him, his task was simple. It was merely
to convince the envoys that Miltiades really was absent
and had not tried to dodge receiving them.

All too soon the envoys appeared, escorted by a rabble
of citizens who pushed inside the throne room in such numbers that Miltiades's scruffy guards were forced to block
the entry. They did not accomplish this without a noisy
struggle. Meanwhile, fresh arrivals outside yelled anxious
questions at their luckier friends within. In fact, the Sestians were too much interested in the affair to show the
least respect for public dignity. Luckily these Persians had

met with Greeks before and did not seem offended. They waited for the excitement to die down, listened to Metiochos stammering through prepared sentences, and made no answer save a slight inclination of the head. Eventually a silence fell. The taller man came forward with his interpreter beside him and spoke in Aramaic.

"These are the words which Darius, son of Hystaspes, the Great King, the King of Kings, the One King of Many, of the family of Achaemenes, the Persian, sends to the tyrant of the Chersonese:

IT IS MY PURPOSE, WITH THE FAVOR OF THE WISE GOD, AHURA MAZDA, TO ENLARGE MY KINGDOM. I WILL MARCH BY SEA AND LAND AGAINST THE SCYTHIANS WHO DWELL NORTH OF THE DANUBE AND INLAND FROM THE BLACK SEA. TO SMOOTH MY WAY THITHER, I WILL TAKE POSSESSION OF THE LANDS LOOKING ON THE GREAT STRAIT. THEREFORE LET MILTIADES, TYRANT OF THE CHERSONESE, DO HOMAGE TO ME. LET HIM SEND ME EARTH AND WATER IN TOKEN THAT HE IS MY SLAVE. AND WHEN I SET FORTH, LET MILTIADES JOIN ME WITH ALL THE SHIPS HE HAS, LEAVING NONE BEHIND."

This message, spoken slowly with pauses for interpretation, was received with silence still as death. When it was over, no one spoke or stirred for a few minutes. Metiochos glanced sideways at his council to see what he must do, but the old men with sunken faces were not looking at him.

"Earth and water!" said one of them in a whisper,

speaking not so much to as for his colleagues. "In token of submission!" His face moved strangely and a slow tear ran down into a wrinkle, where it hung as if frozen. "Earth and water!"

No one else said anything. The people in the throne room might have been mourners at a death bed. Oh, Sestos would always look the same! Fire and sword would not sweep through its streets. Its men and women would not be carried into slavery. Their little temple, which was half-finished now, would go on adding stone to stone. But something had gone from them all. The people would never crowd again into the throne room as though what happened there was everyone's business. Decisions would be made a long way off. Miltiades would be no longer the ruler whom they had chosen themselves. The Persians would keep him in office for their own reasons and as long as he pleased them. The town would never quarrel with its rivals in the strait, stand up to hard knocks or drive close bargains with them. The Sestians were like householders with fierce pride in their homes who found themselves tenants.

Every man seemed to mourn by himself. Even those in the courtyard had understood the news without need of telling. They stood quietly in the dust and the bright sun, a shabby people in a dingy little town of ramshackle buildings which used to be alive. In spirit, it was finished because it pleased the Great King to enlarge his kingdom.

Metiochos, conspicuous on his bare throne, had a lump in his throat. His voice would not come out of him except as a hoarse squeak. He gulped and swallowed. Miltiades was still the leader of these men. He must speak for his father.

"There is not any man," he said at last, flushing scarlet as he heard his voice in the silence, "who can give you earth and water, save Miltiades. We have sent for him, and in the meanwhile we offer the Persian lords our hospitality."

He meant that of some wealthy man, not his own. But no one answered.

The Petition

MILTIADES came riding back to his dominions, dust-covered and grim. He gave earth and water. For that time the Persians departed, passing up the strait in the direction of Lampsacos and the other cities along it. In a little while, not much seemed altered. Children played in the dusty streets. Goats went out to pasture. Men lounged on the waterfront while ships came in. Melissa, who had been left behind at Thrace, returned with her children and was accompanied by King Oloros. The Thracian kingdom extended from the Black Sea to the North Aegean. The Great King could march no army up to the Danube without crossing Oloros's borders, and yet no envoys had been sent to ask his submission.

Oloros, smooth as ever, showed little alarm. It was easy for his semi-nomad people to burn their villages, collect their cattle, and take refuge inland. Scythia, meanwhile, was wild country. Its inhabitants were numerous and warlike. Oloros knew them well, and he promised that they would teach the Great King to respect them.

Meanwhile, he lingered on the coast, collecting all the news which came into Sestos. Nor did he omit to praise Metiochos for all that he had done to represent his father. Indeed, he made so much of the summer's events that Miltiades looked like a thundercloud, while his council whispered they had been wrong to bring the boy forward.

Melissa, far more open in her ways, was frankly jealous. The Chersonese belonged to her own son. She jumped to the conclusion that Metiochos had been left behind that summer on purpose to make him conspicuous. She teased Miltiades to send him back to Athens and sulked when he told her that with Hippias in his present state of suspicion, no one's life was safe there.

Metiochos himself was hardly affected by jealous undercurrents. Among the Athenian exiles who had lately fled to Sestos was young Conon from Marathon, a friend of his own age. The pair of them spent little time inside the palace and none in the women's quarters. Metiochos had grown out of Melissa. With the heedlessness of youth, he never considered that she would have forgiven him if he had been willing to dawdle about with her as he once used to.

It was soon late in the summer. Evenings drew in early. Metiochos was walking home in the dusk, as he now often did, when he remembered that he had promised to leave word with a captain about a sword which he had thought of buying, since people said that weapons would be scarce by spring. As the thought came to him, he turned sharp around on his heel. The sudden movement brought him face to face with a figure behind him who had actually raised a knife in his hand. For a half second, the two stood motionless facing each other, both paralyzed by the emergency.

They moved at the same moment. The knife descended even as Metiochos twisted violently sideways, catching at his attacker's arm. He broke the force of the blow, but could not prevent the point, which was razor-sharp, from lodging in his shoulder. He staggered back a pace, blood running down his arm. He called out loudly. As a shout answered him, his assailant left the weapon in the wound and fled down an alley.

Miltiades looked black indeed when his son was brought in wounded from outside his very door. He took the knife in his hand and turned it over, remarking it was of Thracian make and that such weapons were common in the town. More than this he would not say in public; but King Oloros brought his visit to an end and rode away, bland as ever.

Melissa of course remained, furiously indignant at the

whispers which went around about her father. Miltiades was at pains to disclaim the slightest suspicion. Oloros was the only man in the world who could protect him against the wrath of the Great King, should it ever happen that the time would be ripe to reassert his freedom. But the more Miltiades pretended that Oloros had gone only because the winter approached, the more Melissa blamed Metiochos for the rumors which she heard. She would scarcely speak to him, and a fresh incident added fuel to her fury.

Confined to the house by his wound, Metiochos took notice of his little sister, who was running freely everywhere, demanding playmates. Pretty soon he was a favorite with her, his arm being little drawback to romps with a three-year-old. Melissa, to whom a girl was of minor importance, showed no disapproval. Presently the alliance drew Metiochos back into the women's quarters.

He had always entered these freely as a son of the house. His recent absence had been of his own free will, and he had not imagined that anything had changed his right of entry. Thus, following his sister, with whom he was playing a game of hide and seek, he came into the courtyard while Melissa's nurse was bathing Cimon. The little girl ran up to her brother, and Metiochos followed. The baby, a large and healthy child, was always in good humor when he was out of his swaddling clothes and able to throw his legs and arms about. He gurgled and grinned as his big brother bent over to tickle his stomach. Indeed, he wriggled so hard that the nurse could not hold him, all wet and slippery as he was. She caught him by the leg as he slid out of her towel. His head fell backwards and banged against the water jar. He set up an immediate howl which brought Melissa running.

It was all Metiochos's fault, she told him furiously. Melissa had a firm belief in the evil eye and was terrified at the exposure of her handsome son, not one year old, without any covers. Crediting her stepson with the jealousy which she felt herself, she blamed him for exciting the child to wriggle out of his wrappings. One accusation led to another. What was he doing in the women's quarters? Flirting with the servant? She would have him know that she was not used to people walking in and out of her private rooms without permission.

Miltiades, to whom she carried her complaints, was at pains to assure her that his son would not disturb her quarters again. Her story of jealous ill-wishing and the evil eye he dismissed as nonsense. As it happened, however, Melissa's superstitious fears were genuine. Her original grievance was hardened by resentment. She went back to her quarters in a silence which was not like her, brooding darkly.

Miltiades did not much care about the trouble in his household. He had serious things on his mind. It was already clear that he and his subjects were caught up in a movement which was too big for them. Miltiades was resigned to the outfitting of his five ships. He now discovered he would have to supply them all summer long, which meant taking freighters in attendance. To draft these from his subjects would ruin many. To load them would strip storehouses bare. Some might imagine that with all the fleets coming up through the straits, the Chersonese would make a fair profit from the war. Miltiades reflected that fighting ships took what they pleased and seldom paid.

All winter long fresh messages came streaming across the straits. Instructions varied between impossible and awkward. Histiaeos, tyrant of Miletos and commander of seventy-five warships, many of them newfangled triremes, had the Persian admiral's ear. He naturally used it to improve his own position and that of his city. Commands too difficult to obey were shunted downward to little tyrants like Miltiades, whose goodwill was not worth having.

A bridge of boats, it was explained, would be constructed for the army across the Bosporos from Asia to Europe. Mandrocles of Samos, the greatest living engineer, was coming in person to supervise the work. Miltiades, whose ships were already bespoken, had now to find others for this mighty project. He gave frantic orders at the shipyard and tore his hair. He doubted whether cables would hold against the current, of whose strength he was a better judge than someone from Samos. If the bridge broke up, his ships would be splintered. If it did not, the Bosporos would be blocked for the whole of the summer. No grain could be shipped from the Black Sea. The towns of the Chersonese had made no pretence of feeding themselves from its unfertile soil. There would be starvation in Sestos next winter, unless Miltiades mistook the matter.

Meanwhile, though Militades cursed and his council looked gloomy, the towns of the Chersonese buzzed with excitement. The young men saw themselves swept into an adventure on a vaster scale than they had ever dreamed of. They could hardly wait for spring as they burnished their armor or flexed their rowing muscles. Boys like Conon were mad with envy of Metiochos because he was to go. His own delight was shown so clearly that Melissa protested he was swollen with conceit.

"He makes you ridiculous," she exclaimed waspishly when Metiochos went out in his armor to get used to wearing it. "What business has a child of fifteen with an expedition of grown men? He should be in the schoolroom."

"Will you never leave the boy alone?" Miltiades growled, but he did consult Cleon.

"Is my son too young for this affair? I hardly wish to leave him all summer long with the daughter of Oloros, who does nothing but find fault."

Cleon pulled at his long nose. "King Darius has left Persia and is marching westward gathering his armies. Has no one told you what he did to one of his nobles?"

"No."

"They say that a man who had three sons in the army came to the king, praying one might stay at home. Darius promised him that all three should remain and dismissed him, rejoicing. Then the king sent executioners and left the boys — dead."

Miltiades bit his lip. "Darius did this to one of his own Persians?"

"So they say."

"Barbarian!" Miltiades's face flushed red with anger.

"If it were only a matter of earth and water and the tribute! But there is no end to the demands of the Great King."

Spring came all too soon, and presently the ships were coming up the strait, each city's contingent decked gaily out with paint. First came the warships, most of these no bigger than Miltiades's own, with fifty rowers, a dozen armed men on deck, and flute-players setting the time. The bigger cities had biremes, nearly twice as large, or even triremes which carried a crew of almost two hundred with oars banked in threes. These came flashing past in fine style, caring little for the current, though they did not row all day because their captains were anxious not to wear out their crews. Behind these straggled the merchant ships, smaller, rounder, and putting into port after lengthy struggles like the tortoise who raced the hare. Some of the captains of these last proved bribable. For a shocking price in silver, an occasional sack of grain found its way into Sestos and vanished into locked storerooms. Miltiades ordered Melissa to let the people hunt salad greens or berries as long as the summer should last, dig crocus bulbs and pull up wild garlic. Let them fish from such boats as they had. The grain was for winter.

Miltiades undertook these transactions himself, spending treasure freely. His ships had all gone ahead to the Bosporos, commanded by Cleon. He chafed at the necessity, well knowing that any contingent whose tyrant was not in the council chamber would get the worst station. But another of those orders which made him so angry had commanded his presence at home until the last moment.

The Great King, whose army was now marching north through Asia Minor, had a fancy to see the straits for himself. He was passing through them by ship and would break his journey at Sestos, where he desired to inspect the narrows. Therefore Miltiades, slave of the Great King, and his immediate household were required to welcome him and do homage in person.

Older people shook heads in dismay, but Conon and the other boys too young for the expedition were wild with excitement at seeing the Great King after all. Even Metiochos agreed that it was some consolation for having the Sestian ships go off without them. Melissa said tartly that warships would be better off without babies in them, but he hardly listened to her nowadays.

He and Conon soon found plenty to watch. A couple of ships arrived, containing Median servants and the campaigning tent of the Great King. Swarming into the marketplace, they started to clear it by piling the booths into a corner and setting them afire. Luckily these were so cheap that even the Sestians regarded the spectacle as well worth the loss.

The tent of the Great King turned out to be an elaborate structure containing an anteroom and inner chamber. The whole was made of a rough linen treated with oils to waterproof it, but inside it was lined with silk and floored with carpets such as the gaping Sestians had never seen.

"Outside of Persia, the King never touches the ground with foot or sandal," said Metiochos, who had picked up this detail from his father.

Conon's eyes bulged. "However does he get about?"

"In a chariot, or they lay down carpets. I suppose he fights on horseback. Many of the Persian noblemen do so."

Conon nudged him. "I should like to see the King's chariot in one of our ravines!" They giggled together.

"They'd make a road for him." Metiochos was sobered by the incredible power of the King. "He could drive anywhere."

There was no answer to this, especially when they saw with what speed the servants worked. The tent was already pitched, and a little forest of smaller ones was springing up around it. The Steward of the King's Water was beginning to oversee the unloading of his skins. The King, said one of the bearers who spoke Greek, would drink no water, save from the Choaspes. He did not relax this custom merely because the Choaspes was three months' journey away in Persia or because he would be absent from it nearly a year. The King's Water Steward was an important man with a vast train of servants, draft animals, and carts at his disposal.

Even Conon looked solemn now. The trouble taken to transport the King's Water from Persia stunned his imagination. It was almost a relief to admire the furniture of the Great King's table, which included his own golden cup and mixing vessels as well as dishes for a banquet. Rejecting with the utmost scorn all rooms in the palace, the Steward of the Tables set these up under silken awnings, screening them from public view by ordering everyone out of the buildings at that end of the market. The empty houses were seized on by the Steward of the Kitchens for storage of his rare wines, dates, figs, and other dainties. Coarser victuals he demanded in quantity from Miltiades.

The Great King himself appeared in a ship of Miletos with Histiaeos, tyrant of that city, by his side and a cluster of Persians behind him. Miltiades tood waiting on the dock with his son beside him and Melissa one step behind. Melissa had defiantly brought her own son to offset Metiochos. She had twisted a gold ribbon in her hair and put around her neck a barbarian ornament of heavy gold and dull green stones. She was not to be awed by the Great King, being the daughter of a great king herself. Miltiades thought things might go better in his absence if the King afforded her some recognition.

Miltiades had set his jaw in a grim expression. He was white with fury and humiliation. The moment the Great King stood on the dock, it would be his duty to fall on his knees and put his face in the dust before everyone, including his family and those of his subjects who could get near enough to have a clear view. He felt that he would never sit at ease in his throne room in front of people who had seen him do such a thing. But there was no help for it.

Strangely enough, when the act was performed, it did not seem so dreadful. The Great King, standing on the carpet which had been laid for him, was neither anxious to spare his subject's feelings nor to triumph. He was simply indifferent to a formality which had long been a matter of course. His eyes calmly rested on Metiochos as the boy made the low bow expected of him, while putting his fingers to his lips. They passed on to Melissa and did, perhaps, linger there. But it was not the custom for the King to acknowledge complimentary gestures, so that he did not so much as move his head in answer to them.

He let Miltiades get up and began at once to ask him questions translated by the tyrant of Miletos. What was the depth of the channel? How deep was the current? How many towns on either side? What sort of harbors? How stormy in the winter season? How many ships put into Sestos yearly? What proportion were they of ships trading with the Black Sea? He would listen to the answer Miltiades gave, nod briefly, and put another question, as though in a hurry to satisfy a ferocious hunger for knowledge.

Forbidden to look the Great King in the face, Miltiades kept eyes discreetly on the ground. Metiochos, in a position to take a more general view, perceived from cautious glances that the Great King was a man of middle height, so broad and burly that he seemed shorter than he was. He had a noble head with a wide forehead, great aquiline nose, and deepset eyes with heavy eyebrows. His beard, of the most magnificent length and thickness, was apparently all his own, though rumor had it that those of eastern kings often were not. Darius looked strong as a bear, and he straddled slightly like a man who spends much time on horseback. His manner was direct and by no means haughty, yet it was evident that by behaving as he pleased he gave no permission for others to do so.

Paying not the smallest heed to the chariot waiting, Darius put out a broad hand down the back of which grew thick black hair, and he beckoned forward one of the Persians in attendance. "Megabazos," said the tyrant of Miletos, "chief general of the King's armies."

Darius gave his decisive little nod and continued to ask questions, while Megabazos, haughtier in manner, looked Miltiades up and down.

The King was passing from the subject of the straits themselves to that of the cities. How many were on the straits? And what size? How many in the Chersonese itself? How big was Sestos? What size was its war fleet? Its trading fleet? The contingent it had sent to the rendezvous? Under the insolent stare of Megabazos, Miltiades had grown red. He did not relish describing the poverty of his dominions in men or ships and money in the hearing of a haughty Persian lord or even of that richest of all tyrants, Histiaeos of Miletos.

The King paused for a moment to look around Sestos, and he took his time to do so, noting the dusty sheds by the docks, the mean and huddled houses, and the lack of pretension everywhere. What sort of land was there in the Chersonese? If so unfertile, what did people live on? What had they to offer in trade? The products of Thrace?

This was very delicate ground, considering the Great King's purpose to cross the lands of Oloros. Miltiades was at pains to answer calmly, but perhaps he did not succeed in this. Darius let his eyes rest casually once more on Melissa. "The daughter of the King of Thrace, or is she not?"

This final question was perhaps more slowly spoken. The King's voice was calm, but Miltiades ran his tongue across his lips and paused a moment. Then, deciding on boldness, he said firmly, "She is indeed the daughter of that king and will govern Sestos when I am with the fleet. Therefore she is your slave, O King of Kings, as I am."

Darius gave his little nod of satisfaction. "A brave woman! Ask her what she requires to lighten her task when you are gone."

There was another stir among the men behind the king. Melissa, flushing scarlet up to the roots of her hair, hesitated, caught utterly aback. Darius waited, conveying by no more than a raising of the eyebrows that he was not a man who was used to being kept waiting.

"She is overwhelmed by the honor done her," said Miltiades in desperation.

Histiaeos did not bother to interpret this to the King, seeing that it was not Miltiades's business to speak unless addressed. But her husband's words seemed to give Melissa courage. She glanced at him and caught sight of Metiochos standing beside him. Her eyes narrowed.

"Grant me my husband's son to stay behind and help me," she said with spite.

The voice of the interpreter faltered, and there was a shocked silence in which Metiochos cried out, "Oh no! Oh no!" in desperate protest. Miltiades, turning his back on the Great King with a contemptuous disregard of etiquette, caught Melissa full across the mouth with his open hand. The blow sounded like a thunderclap. Melissa fell back with a cry and covered her face.

"The petition is granted," said the King in his accented Greek.

His voice was quiet, but Miltiades felt his blood run cold. He could see that Histiaeos was looking at him with pity in his eyes. He wondered who were the Great King's executioners.

"O King," he spread his hands like a petitioner, "like all your judgments, this is just. The boy is only fifteen and cannot come. He is not strong enough to pull an oar, while my little ships have room for no one else save a few picked fighters. Let him stay behind, O King, as you have said — but not in Sestos, where the Princess has a son of her own to keep her company. I did intend him to command my ships in the Bosporos which are part of the great bridge. Indeed, I have no one else, for all my best men come with me."

The King looked darkly at Metiochos. He seemed to consider.

"Very well," he said at last. "The boy stays at the Bosporos. As for your woman, you may tell her she is a fool. She should have asked for food."

The Bridge

METIOCHOS was indignant with Melissa for spoiling his summer. He did not understand what she meant when she wept and told his father that she had not known what she was doing. Miltiades did not enlighten his son, but he made Melissa swear a fearsome oath by all his gods and hers, praying to them that her son might never rule the Chersonese if she plotted more harm against his. He had not leisure to do more, for the Great King's curiosity had transferred itself to the Sea of Marmora, which lay between the Chersonese straits and those of the Bosporos. It was time to follow.

The fleet was already assembled in the magnificent harbor on the European side of the Bosporos, while the army's campfires lit up the Asian sky across half a mile of water. Two enormous ropes were stretched across the strait; but the ships which were to form the bridge were not all in position. Those of Miltiades, as their ruler had foreseen, had been commandeered early, with the result that one had been crushed when the attachment of the cables on the eastern shore had given way. The remaining three were now in place, moored at an angle which minimized the force of the current. Their crews, about sixty men, were camping ashore with the rowers of the warships, sharing their rations. Their labor had been drafted onto the rafts and smaller boats which were rowing people, brushwood, stores and extra cable in this direction or that amid general cursing.

Miltiades put the boy in command straightaway. He was no help at heavy labor, but his presence protected his men from exploitation. The tyrant of Lampsacos, who was a big bullying man and lately married to a daughter of Hippias of Athens, demanded the use of a boatload of Metiochos's men because he was shorthanded. Metiochos could retort that the tyrant of Miletos, to whom he was well known, had sent them with a message to Mandrocles. On receiving this, the great engineer dispatched him with orders to those who were stretching ships' sails on either side of the boat-bridge, lest horses and camels go mad with fear when they see the water beneath them. Mandrocles was hot and hoarse and almost melting with fury at the clumsiness of ill-managed ships and the stupidity of captains. When he saw that the screening went on better, he adopted Metiochos as messenger, allowing him a couple of boats which his men manned in relays. Gratefully they stood up for him as he gave orders to truculent people who were more than twice his age. Long before the bridge was ready for crossing, his men had forgotten what they said among themselves when he was put over them.

The disadvantage of working directly with the engineer of the bridge was that Mandrocles drove himself from dawn to dark and Metiochos was forced to do the same. It was not easy to get attention paid to orders when a hundred and fifty ships were clogging the fairway belonging to thirty independent cities, each determined that its people should do no more work than the others. Metiochos's head soon buzzed with fatigue. His voice grew as hoarse as Mandrocles's own. He learned to crowd his boat with men and arm them with stout sticks to make them respected.

After days of struggle, the cables were properly tightened and all the ships were in place. The actual roadway, which was being laid down from both ends, was nearing the middle. Mandrocles had retreated to a tiny promontory on the eastern side which overlooked the whole length, and whence he could measure progress by the heads of toiling men as they appeared above the screens. Great numbers were employed on the work, and it was proceeding at considerable speed. Mandrocles had twice promised the

King that the crossing could soon start and twice postponed it. He was biting his fingers with impatience as he moved up and down in front of a half-dozen Persian commanders, who were waiting to give orders to the army.

"Work's stopped on the western side," he snapped, visibly fuming. "Not a load has come up for the last ten minutes. Lazy dogs! Here, you, go see what's the matter!"

He gestured at Metiochos, who jumped down from the rock on which they were standing and dashed toward the beach. He had discovered that messages must be taken at full tilt. The moment he disappeared from Mandrocles's side, his men would tumble into the boat which they held ready. The oarsmen took their places on the thwarts, while two or three others waited knee-deep in the water to push off the moment Metiochos stumbled aboard.

It was easy to see what the trouble was as they drew nearer. Men had been carrying the dirt for the roadway down to the middle of the bridge by oxcart. Empty carts returning had hardly room to pass those coming up. Perhaps a drover had not been skillful with his animals, or possibly a swinging horn had ripped the screen aside, exposing the sea. At all events, a half-dozen carts, some full of dirt, were locked in confusion with splintered wheels and broken poles. Their oxen, backing uneasily from a great hole in the screening, were shifting as the decks moved, doing further damage to the bulwarks and screens or to the carts in the roadway. Meanwhile, on either side of this obstruction, other carts were halted which could not be turned around on the bridge without unyoking their oxen.

Around these crowded the laborers who were spreading the dirt, prolonging a break in their hard work by obstructing the passage of anyone in authority.

Metiochos brought the boat alongside and scrambled onto the bridge through the gap in the screening, which was large enough to suggest that a cart and its oxen had crashed into the sea. He did not waste time shouting orders to the drovers, but turned to his men, who swung in after him. He pointed to the broken carts. "Get these loose from their animals and throw them over the side!"

"Not so fast!" One of the drovers was a thickset, shaggy man with a scar on his cheek. He raised his ox-goad, a heavy stick with a wicked-looking point of iron. "We'll sort our carts out in our own way."

"That's right," agreed another.

"Go home and grow your beard! Interfering between a man and his cart!" The shaggy man made his goad whistle through the air in a threatening motion. Behind him a murmur seemed to agree that the best things to put in the water were the foreign boy and his boat's crew.

Metiochos, who had faced similar scenes for several days, was too tired to be patient. "Mandrocles sent me, you fools! If any of you has long sight, you can see him on the headland, as clearly as he can see you." He remembered the Persians standing behind Mandrocles and improvised rapidly. "Perhaps your vision is good enough to distinguish the Great King beside him. If you keep the King waiting, you'll be lucky to escape with your lives, losing oxen and carts." He advanced roughly on the shaggy yokel and pushed him aside with his hand. "Get those carts over!"

By the time he returned to Mandrocles an hour later, the work was proceeding on both sides of the bridge as busily as ever. "A blockage," he explained. "We tipped the carts into the water, and when they were out of the way we could manage the oxen."

Mandrocles was still fuming. "An hour's work lost! Why could they not clear it themselves?"

Metiochos shrugged wearily. His eyes were almost swollen shut from sheer fatigue. He blinked at Mandrocles. "Well, the drovers owned the oxen and the carts. They were poor men."

Mandrocles gave a short bark of laughter. Behind him a voice only too well remembered asked a question in Aramaic. With a start of horror, Metiochos realized he was in the presence of the Great King. Mandrocles translated. "Who were these peasants with their carts and oxen?"

Metiochos made a hasty reverence and stammered that all the oxen came from Byzantium and the cities hereabout. Realizing that this fell short of the definite answer which Darius seemed to expect, he added that he had made no inquiries because of his haste to get the work resumed. He had no more than a dozen men at his back. If he had not hustled the peasants, they probably would have thrown him overboard.

Darius made a gesture of dismissal with one finger. Metiochos tried to fade into the background, hoping that the King had not known who he was, since he seemed displeased. But afterwards Mandrocles said to him, "The King left this medallion for the son of Miltiades, so that when he goes on errands, it may be known he represents the King." It was a circular gold piece with a head of Darius, which hung from a linked chain. Metiochos remembered that though the Great King gathered an immense amount of information daily, people said that he never forgot what he once learned.

On the following morning very early, the bridge being now ready, Darius made sacrifice to Ahura Mazda, the All-Wise. He caused incense to be burned to purify the air from evil spirits. The crossing then commenced, while King Darius took his seat on a reviewing stand to watch the procession.

Two days and nights the army took to cross, while it seemed to the watchers as though all Asia was pouring into Europe. In front marched the foot soldiers, headed by the ten thousand Immortals, who were armored in metal scales sewn onto leather tunics and carried spears with pomegranates on the butts made of silver or gold. Indeed, the Immortals flashed with gold, from the sheaths of their short swords, the buckles of their belts, the chains about their necks, and the discs on their headdresses which had been awarded for special service. Behind them followed their baggage, borne on the backs of donkeys, camels and porters.

After the Immortals came the light-armed troops in irregular masses, good enough to use as a screen for breaking the force of a charge. Each contingent was under a native chief who took his orders from a Persian officer in charge of his section. Most of these carried bows and arrows. Their armor varied from skin cloaks and shields of hide to shields of wicker and quilted corselets stuffed with linen or cotton.

Behind these inferior troops marched the body of the army, composed of Persians, Medians, and kindred people. These were sturdy, sallow-skinned men in leather tunics and loose trousers with great bows slung on their backs, spears in their hands, and swords at their girdles. Amid them rode the Great King himself in a chariot. Before him went the holy chariot of Ahura Mazda, drawn by eight white horses. It was empty, except for the unseen god, of whom there was no image. The charioteer walked behind it, holding the reins.

Next followed the mass of the baggage train with the camp servants, men and women. This took endless hours to cross, though those in charge of it lashed on the stragglers, both men and beasts.

The cavalry, which came last, contained the nobleman of the Medes and Persians, richly clad and followed closely by their personal attendants and even litters in which they brought their favorite wives to share their dangers. With them, the mightiest army which the East had ever seen crossed into Europe, and disappeared toward Thrace, where King Oloros had already denuded his coast of men and cattle. With the army went the main fleet, which would be needed for bridging the Danube. Even Mandrocles was taken away by Darius to see to this work. A great quiet settled over the blue waters of the Bosporos and over its dusty shores. Fifteen hundred people remained encamped with no duties, save to strengthen the cables of the bridge against freak storms.

Metiochos soon discovered that war waged on a vast scale could be dull. His men lounged and cursed. Entertainers had flocked across with the army in great numbers, and some of them had remained by the bridge. But to Metiochos's youthful view, one Egyptian dancing girl was much like another. He preferred to pick up Aramaic from the pedlars who swarmed through the camp with dubious wares.

After about three weeks, the Great King's army was considered far enough off to be no present problem. Lycophron of Miletos, who commanded the greatest number of ships, took it on himself to summon a council. Why should they not open the straits to trade? This would be possible if a few end ships were removed. The great cables had been secured to headlands and then tightened with enormous capstans until their outer ends hung free of the water.

Metiochos, representing the Chersonese, said nothing at this meeting. All the captains present were twice his age. Many of them had been deliberately left behind by their own tyrants because they were suspected of opposition. Metiochos had already perceived that the Great King's medallion, which he wore about his neck, made him unpopular. Since he dared not take it off, lest this be reported, he kept to himself as much as he could in his own quarters. Here he summoned the captains of his ships to discuss the decision of the council.

"They must release our two end ships," he pointed out, "not out of goodwill, but because of their position."

The three captains nodded, taking time to consider. Nicanor, who was the oldest, deliberately bent down, selecting a piece of grass to chew. He thrust it into his mouth and bit at it. When the juice had been extracted to his satisfaction, he said slowly, "There is a ship of Athens waiting to pass the Bosporos. I talked with its captain, who spent a night in Sestos. The Princess has ordered the public granaries opened already."

Nicander gave a preliminary grunt. "It'd not take above a few weeks to get grain from Sinope and run it back through the straits. The King's at the Danube."

Niceratos shrugged heavy shoulders. "Those Asia Minor Greeks would never let us go. I said to that Athenian, 'You're wasting your time,' I said. 'They're not calling a council to open the straits for men from the mainland. Grain'll be carried by Ephesos, Miletos, and the others. Make up your mind to that,' I said." He spat.

The problem having been thus defined, there was a long silence. Metiochos broke it by suggesting his ships should sail without permission. He thought he could contrive to get them away.

"They'd have to pass the Bosporos on the journey home," Niceratos pointed out. "They'd never do it."

Nicander grunted again in agreement. Nicanor said nothing.

"We could at least land our grain here," Metiochos urged. "When the bridge breaks up at the end of the season, we can carry it home."

Niceratos, who had assumed the role of spokesman, shook his head. If it was known they had extra supplies, these would certainly be taken when other people ran short.

Nicander agreed. There was little to gamble with or pay the hire of dancing girls except one's rations.

"In any case, when the army comes back, it will seize everything," Niceratos grunted.

This seemed too probable to be denied. There was another silence, lasting a full five minutes. From the headland where they were sitting, they had a good view of the bridge, rocking gently in the swell.

Nicanor took the grass out of his mouth and nodded two or three times to himself, as though he had made up his mind. "No need to bring the grain back here. Just bury it quietly in a convenient cove. All the shore of Thrace is empty of people. Pick it up in half a day before we go home."

"If we come back here empty-handed, people will guess."

Nicanor pursed his lips. "Pirates! Chased by pirates! Had to jettison most of our cargo to get away. Bring in a little."

Nicander slapped his hand on his thigh and started to laugh.

The gap in the bridge was made next day, and the ships released from it were beached in the harbor. Lycophron appointed guards to be sure that they were ready to take up their position again at a moment's notice. Metiochos made no protest. He spread the news around that he planned a party.

Celebrations, increasingly noisy and wild, were becoming common among those who could hire the dancing girls and their musicians. Torches would be set up for the show, and wine would flow freely. Presently drunken yells would punctuate the clashing of cymbals. On this occasion, neighbors who drifted over to share the fun found the men of the Chersonese quite out of hand. Metiochos himself was dancing with the girls, flinging up his legs with a wild abandon which was hardly decent for a boy his age. It surprised no one when he staggered off into the night and did not return. New arrivals kept the total numbers high when others followed.

The guards of the beach blinked at Metiochos, who had come down to them at a run followed by his people. He held out the King's medallion. "A message from Susa arrived for the King. Let my men past."

The captain of the guard hesitated. He had only to set up a yell and summon reinforcements. But he knew Metiochos, as did all who had worked on the bridge. He had seen him running around with orders. He had heard the story of the Great King's medal. Messages for the King came all the way from Susa at full gallop by the hands of relays of horsemen. They arrived by day or night, and it was a capital crime to delay them a minute.

The ships went out; and Lycophron raged, the more so because other people laughed. Metiochos protested that the ships were his own and he had not been forbidden to use them, which was perfectly true, since he had never asked permission. He was ready to promise that they would be back with their cargoes before they were needed.

This incident made Metiochos remarkable to many who had thought him recommended to the great ones by nothing but good looks. People whispered about him as he strolled through the camp. Men who were jealous of the Milesians took him up and soon reported him wise beyond his years. No doubt they made much of little in order to annoy Lycophron, but their flattery began to be noticeable to the boy himself. He was frightened at it, perceiving that he was being used.

"That pretty boy! That tyrant's son!" raged Lycophron to his friends. "I wish we were rid of him."

Demonax, who was the leader of the Ephesian contingent, looked doubtful. "Miltiades is on our side."

"A tyrant! Who told you so?"

"Cleon."

Lycophron paced up and down. "You all trust Cleon."

"We all know him."

"Like half the captains of the fleet. It was sheer madness for Cleon to sail with them. Someone has betrayed him to the Persians. There's no message."

"There will be."

On the very next day fifty ships came in from the Danube to fetch supplies which the army would need when it returned. They had sailed two days' journey up the river and found a place to bridge. The army had crossed and disappeared into wild country. Nothing more was likely to be heard for another month.

"There was a word," said Demonax into Lycophron's ear.

"What was it?"

"Patience."

More than a month passed without further message, during which rumors began to circulate that King Darius was cut off with his army north of the Danube. Each had his own version of this tale. None knew quite where it came from.

"Soothsayers!" Lycophron said darkly over his wine. "Telling people what they want to hear! The purest invention!"

Demonax tossed the dregs of his cup with a flick of the wrist, and he hit the bowl he had aimed for. "Look at that hit! My luck's in! There are impostors among soothsayers, but I could tell you stories . . ."

"I want a message from the Danube," Lycophron persisted.

Metiochos had heard the rumors, too. He told Niceratos, who had returned by now, that they came from the Thracians. "Their traders are drifting back," he pointed out. "Many speak Greek."

Niceratos rubbed the back of his neck and supposed that the Thracians knew what was going on. They had neighbors on the Danube. Metiochos was not so sure. He wondered if these fabrications might not be traced to the cautious hand of King Oloros.

By now it was said that Darius and his army were lost for good. Captains were heard to mutter that their ships ought to be released from the bridge before the season was over. Why keep them tied up until it was too late for trade?

Metiochos became alarmed. "Did you ever imagine," he said to his own captains, "being shut up in a cage with a raging lion? If these Asiatics go home, the Great King's army will find itself cut off in Europe. How can we then protect the Chersonese?"

This was a terrifying thought, but the three captains were half convinced themselves that Darius was already defeated. The story current now declared that there had been a great battle in Scythia and the vultures had been gorged with heaps of the slain. The head of Darius grinned, eyeless, from a tree where the victors had nailed it.

At last a ship came in from the fleet on the Danube. Cleon, who commanded it in person, brought it into harbor by night. He left his rowers, who had pushed themselves to the limit of their strength, to rest on the beach, while he went up to Lycophron. The calling of a council was cried through the camp at dawn before the people had time to realize that their waiting was over. Metiochos, seating himself on the bank of the grassy hollow in which the meeting was held, had no notion that Cleon was the messenger until he saw him.

Cleon looked thinner and browner than ever. His cloak, slept in all summer, was positively ragged. But he threw it back from his shoulders with an air and called out to the people, "The king of Persia," he made the gesture of cutting his throat, "is dead. His army," he snapped his fingers, "is scattered like mist. The Danube bridge is breaking up. The Persian survivors will be trapped. Greeks, we are free!" He spread both hands in a triumphant gesture while the captains rose with a roar. People slapped each other on the shoulders, did little dances, clasped hands, shook fists, and went through all the gestures that men make at a moment of excitement.

"Down with all tyrants!" cried a voice. There was a hubbub of applause.

"We knew it weeks ago," shouted Cleon, dominating the tumult while he gestured to the people to sit down. "The Thracians told us. But Histiaeos and the tyrants, who depend on the King, held the people in check; and none dared move. Six days ago, when the King had already been absent for sixty without any tidings, we saw smoke of campfires. Our hearts sank. But it was an army of Scythians which came rolling down toward our bridge on their shaggy horses. Those who were anchored near the far bank had to pull out of line, lest they be stormed and set afire.

"There was clamor to go home. Histiaeos called a council to discuss with his friends how they might best control the people. But even here one of the tyrants spoke out bravely for freedom, telling the others that the King would be destroyed if the bridge were broken. The council broke up in confusion with nothing accomplished. Then, perceiving how the matter must go, I sailed for the Bosporos to tell you that you are free."

Cheering and shouting broke out again and seemed as though it would never stop. People's faces were red, and their eyes shone with tears. They grimaced at one another and doubled up with fits of laughter at nothing. They fell into each other's arms in sudden embraces.

Lycophron came forward to Cleon's side and started to motion for silence. Then he made the people sit down again.

"Let us all give our opinions," he said, "on what ought to be done. I will call a roll of the commanders. First, however, lest any think that I hang back, I will give my vote for breaking the bridge and will add to it a demand of my own." He drew himself up and called out in a loud voice, "Down with Histiaeos, tyrant of Miletos. The people will govern themselves!"

This raised another outcry. When Lycophron began to call the roll, starting with Demonax, it soon appeared that he had set a fashion. Every man voted for the breaking of the bridge and added something which the day before he would have been afraid to utter. People called for the downfall of their particular tyrant by name, hoped for democracy, or proposed a free league of all the cities of the Greeks against the Persian. Every utterance earned cheers. The proceedings of the council were supposed to be private, but the noise attracted a ring of auditors whom no one thought to send away. Revolutionary ardor amounting to frenzy swept caution aside.

Metiochos sat still, his eyes on Cleon. The boy was sweating. He rubbed his hands on his tunic because they were sticky. His name would soon be called. He must give his opinion before this frantic crowd. He alone was a tyrant's son, and he did not believe in democracy for the Chersonese. It was different in Athens.

He knew Cleon better than most people. He had heard him by the docks at Sestos let drop information which had been carefully doctored. Cleon hated the Persians.

The rumors from Thrace were ugly, too. Why had they started so early before there was much chance of their being true? It would suit King Oloros if the Greeks and the Scythians ruined Darius. Oloros would desire the bridges to be broken, no matter what happened later to the Greeks.

"Metiochos, son of Miltiades," Lycophron called.

Metiochos stood up amid what seemed a deathlike hush. He could feel sweat run down his forehead.

"When the Danube bridge is broken," he said in his clear carrying voice, "its ships will return. I vote we keep our bridge until they do so."

"Yah, tyrant!"

"Tyrant's son!"

The mood of exaltation was broken. People were angry. A man jumped to his feet and swung at Metiochos, catching him across the lips and jarring his teeth. No single vote had been given for the keeping of the bridge except by the boy who wore the portrait of the Great King around his neck.

"Traitor!"

"Slave!"

Metiochos spat out blood. His lips were swollen and he did not try to speak. He had said enough and knew he would be lucky if he escaped with no worse damage. He glanced about him, decided the spectators formed too close a ring for escape, and stood his ground.

"I command the Chersonese contingent! Let the child alone!" Cleon came stalking through the crowd, pushing people out of his way. He walked forward until he was face to face with the boy. Metiochos in a sullen silence would not look at him, but they stood opposite each other for a few seconds. Then Cleon put out a long arm and lifted off the Great King's medal from the boy's neck. He threw it away. "A little flattery has tamed you," he said. "I thought better of you."

He turned his back on the boy and addressed the crowd. "Which tyrant do you suppose it was who spoke for freedom? It was Miltiades! I give his vote for breaking the bridge. Let us start on the work!"

The meeting began to break up as council and people surged down towards the strait. Men parted on either side of Metiochos, avoiding contact with scornful looks. They left him standing alone on the shore, hands clenched and scowling. None of these fools were rulers. None considered that it was the duty of a tyrant's son to think for his people.

The Crossing

Two DAYS sufficed to tear down the bridge which had taken many to build. Though its ships needed repair, their commanders were burning to get the squadrons away. They saw themselves as leaders of revolution at home. Their success depended on outstripping their tyrants and contingents from the Danube. In a very short time, the straits were bare of shipping. Nothing was left to show for the summer but trampled ground, burned-out campfires, broken potsherds, brushwood shelters, flies and dirt.

Cleon himself was in no hurry. He daily expected the Danube fleet and Miltiades with it. Under Miltiades, he hoped to rally the ships against Histiaeos and other tyrants. Without the war fleet, no struggle could be kept up against the Persian. Cleon was depending on the shock of finding the Bosporos abandoned and learning that revolutions were breaking out at home.

Cleon lingered, waiting for the fleet and detaining the ships of the Chersonese under his command. He had posted scouts to the westward, fearing that the fleet might be so close on his heels that it would catch up with the Bosporos squadrons before their departure. When nothing arrived, he sighed with relief. But after six more days when no sails had appeared, he began to look grim. There had been a delay, and he could think of no explanation which was welcome.

Metiochos, meanwhile, sulked. He would not speak to Cleon and scowled at the captains for obeying him. Yet he too was anxious at the fleet's delay. Mainly because he could not bear to wait, he decided to go with Nicander and Niceratos to recover their grain from the Thracian coast. Cleon raised no obstacle. The boy could do no harm, but he was a nuisance. Let him go.

They sailed two days up the coast of Thrace and spent a couple more loading. There was no hurry. This successful operation broke down the barriers between Metiochos and the men. He gave no orders, but his gloom relaxed a little; and the captains treated him with deference.

They sailed back most of a day and put in early to cook

and camp for the night because the captains knew of a convenient cove. Thus it was not nearly dark when one of the oarsmen who was cutting brush for the campfire came racing down. "Sails!"

Everybody ran to look. There were indeed sails, but moving too fast for any breeze. Only a warship's banks of oars could have commanded such a speed. As they stood watching, more sails appeared behind the first in irregular columns, not quite careless of order, yet foreseeing no need to keep a strict formation. Who was there in the sea to challenge this fleet?

Niceratos pounded Metiochos on the shoulder, so great was his relief. "They've come at last! I was fearing . . ."

Metiochos nodded. His own heart leaped too, and yet the fleet's appearance was no explanation of its delay. Well, soon they would know.

"They'll put in for the night," he said, breaking his self-imposed rule to say nothing not strictly necessary.

"They're making for our cove," Nicander agreed. "No need to use the oars in such a breeze unless they want to reach some spot by dark. There's room for all their ships at once, and there's good water."

He turned back to the cove and issued orders. There was plenty to be done. Neither of the captains had any illusions about the behavior of the crews of warships. The fleet would demand the best places in the bay or on the shore. It was only sensible to shift quarters before being forced to.

By the time they had made these arrangements, the leading triremes were putting in toward the bay. Presently they came swooping down between the headlands, their oars flashing as they crossed the path of the setting sun. The nearest leader was quick to spot the two ships, and someone with a bull-like voice appeared on its prow, agog for news.

"Who-o are you? Where from?"

"Bo-osporos!" yelled Niceratos at the top of his voice. "You're la-ate! We looked for you day-ays ago!"

"Not la-ate!" replied the voice, a little nearer now. "Sent on ahe-ad! Army's two weeks march behind us!"

Niceratos, quite red with the effort of yelling, turned almost pale. "Did you hear that? The army!"

The voice from the trireme shouted another inquiry, but Niceratos did not answer. He turned his back on the shore, repeating, "The army is two weeks' march away . . . and may the gods help us!"

Metiochos, losing his presence of mind altogether, cried out in schoolboy fashion, "I told you so!"

Nicander shook his head in solemn gloom. The three stared at one another while the crews appeared to wait for a suggestion. Nobody had one.

Miltiades had spoken up in council for the breaking of the Danube bridge, and had behind him the sentiment of the fleet. But Histiaeos, rallying the other tyrants, had stood out obstinately, supported by his own captains and those whose fortunes depended on their local rulers. The issue was deadlocked for a night and a day, while the Scythians prowled the farther bank, from which the end ships had been removed.

On the second night, persistent hailing from the bank was answered by the fleet. Darius's vanguard, brushing the Scythians aside like chaff, had reached the Danube, only to find the bridge apparently gone. Next morning they would have seen their error, but their haste was great. The Scythians, though they would not face a charge, hung around the army on its march like buzzing flies. Sick and wounded had been abandoned once, and there were now many more. In particular, the irregular, light-armed troops had been a failure.

Megabazos, who commanded the van, had set people shouting in case the bulk of the bridge had not been removed. When this proved to be the case, it was only the work of a few hours to restore it completely. By dawn, the first of the army had started to cross.

The defeat of Darius, if defeat it actually was, had not been disastrous. There had been hard fighting and dangerous moments when supplies had been cut off or narrow defiles had threatened entrapment. Yet the army was still immense. Megabazos with the bulk of it would winter in Thrace. The Great King in person with the Immortals and perhaps as many more was returning to Asia across the Bosporos bridge — or so he intended.

The news which was now exchanged was welcome to no one. All the tyrants wished to sail home at once and put down revolution. Miltiades, whom they avoided as a ruined man, was so furiously angry that he seemed to give little thought to his own future.

"Let me get my hands on Cleon!" he raged. "I gave

him refuge when people warned that he was dangerous. Now his intrigues have destroyed me."

He raged, but was not allowed to proceed. In a hasty conference of tyrants, Histiaeos persuaded them to send a message to the King. Darius must be as anxious as they to forestall a general rebellion, even if it meant that he must linger in Thrace. The Great King's answer was that he would march on Sestos and cross by the narrows there, lengthening his journey in Europe and shortening it in Asia. By the time that he arrived, the ships of Sigeum, Abydos, Lampsacos, and all other cities near the strait must be there to assist him. The rest might go home.

No sooner had this permission come than there was a rush for the ships. Each separate contingent was anxious to be the first to get away. Miltiades alone had given no orders. He looked silently at his son, serious and questioning. The boy's face had lost its youthful roundness. There was a hardening of the square jaw, a hollowing of the cheeks. The nose was becoming high-bridged, imperious. The lips were narrow and firm. He was taller than his father.

"I shall have to go to Thrace," Miltiades said. Metiochos nodded. He had already perceived that the only refuge left was King Oloros.

Miltiades approved of his son. It pleased him that the boy should have given thought to his situation and yet asked no questions.

"I shall leave you in Sestos," he said. "The Great King owes you something for trying to save his bridge. Besides, Nicander says you will do well."

It was a measure of how much the boy had grown up during the summer that he accepted leadership as his right, neither blushing nor protesting. He merely replied, "I saw Byzantium after the army went through. At Sestos they will be angry, and things will be worse."

"You had better get the women and children into the hills," Miltiades agreed.

It was one thing, as Metiochos found at the end of that summer, to foresee trouble coming. When it arrived, no preparations could avert it. Left by Miltiades in command, he did his best. He set the people to constructing extra rafts and boats, foreseeing that the transport of twenty thousand warriors with their animals, servants, and baggage would take considerable time. Few ships could carry fifty men besides their rowers.

Proclamations had been made that women and children should be sent out of town, that silver should be buried and valuables hidden. But some were sick, and some too old to move. Many people imagined that because they were poor, they were not worth plundering. Meanwhile, in the small farms outside the city, grain had been gathered, but vines and olives were not yet ripe. Goats had often been kept at home for want of anyone to herd them elsewhere. There was plenty that angry men could damage if they had a mind to.

Melissa was ready to leave when her son Cimon, who had never been sick before, succumbed to a fever. Immediately she prepared to stay and nurse him. It ill became her, she added, tossing her head, that she, a daughter of kings, should flee from foreign soldiers, leaving her child in their hands. In vain Metiochos repeated Milti-ades's commands. She sniffed contemptuously and said that her husband need send her no messages through a mere boy. She knew her duty.

Helpless, Metiochos set guards on the palace and hoped that Melissa's rank would protect her from insult. Privately he could not help admiring her. Melissa had stuck a dagger in her girdle, remarking that anyone who laid a hand on her would get it in the ribs. With this simple precaution, she dismissed Darius's army as unimportant compared to Cimon's needs. She had no time for it.

The troops came into the town in excellent order. Darius rode in the midst of them, and the golden chariot of Ahura Mazda still went before him, though drawn by four white horses instead of eight. The beards of his soldiers were shaggy now, their hair long. They had less gold to display. The spears of the Immortals were as often as not plain ones, and some of them were of captured Scythian make. Dirty bandages were to be seen and ragged clothing. But they did not look like defeated men as they came marching down to the docks, where a flotilla of rafts and boats of all sizes awaited them.

All went well for about an hour. Captains of tens and captains of hundreds had their men well in hand. They came down to the docks in excellent order and started to embark. But behind the first arrivals, less disciplined troops pressed into Sestos, accompanied by the drovers of baggage animals and the camp servants. Those who had no chance of getting across before nightfall considered themselves as quartered in the town. They began to make their way into shops or dwellings, pilfering what they could and demanding refreshments. Where they suspected a householder had hidden his valuables, they would threaten him with spears. Little violence actually occurred because the town was nearly empty, but destruction and plundering increased. There was also dysentery among the troops, so that people's dwellings were fouled by the filth of men and animals.

Melissa was unconscious of rising tumult. Her child was very hot, and she had wrapped him in wet cloths to cool him down. She rocked him in her arms and sang to him, fanned off flies, surrounded his bed with lucky charms. She had sent her maids away with her little girl. There was no one with her but an elderly man-slave to fetch her water. All afternoon the boy tossed and wailed and, though he sipped some of her potions, grew no better.

The palace, being the most considerable of the houses in the town, was marked for plunder. Metiochos had placed guards outside it with strict instructions. They were to turn away all who sought an entry as long as they could without a fight. But sooner than come to blows, they were to throw open the throne room and adjacent court, taking up new positions in the doorway leading to the women's quarters. From here they were to dispatch one of their number to warn Metiochos, who was down by the docks. He would appeal at once for Melissa's protection to whatever Persian general he could find.

Unfortunately, when a message did come from the palace, Metiochos was not directing operations. He had been summoned in haste to the temple of Athene, which was a humble structure but did contain vessels of silver offered by rescued sea captains. Thus the soldiers who had pressed into the palace were soon followed by others. They spread out through the rooms until once more they came up against the guards.

Common soldiers as these intruders were, they had no business with princes; but the appearance and furnishings of the palace had been disappointing. The very presence of guards in the entryway suggested there were treasures in the inmost parts of the house. One of the captains of tens who had come in with his men pushed up against the guards, who, uncertain what they should do in the last resort, gave way. The soldiers came noisily into the women's court and looked around it.

Cimon had fallen into an uneasy sleep. Melissa started up from his side in indignation and went out into the court. Melissa was dressed as Miltiades liked to see her, in Ionian fashion. The ends of her loose robe were caught together over her shoulders and down her arms with clasps of gold. The fine linen, damp with the cloths of the boy she had been holding, clung close to her, revealing more than she usually showed to strangers, more especially because, being in her private rooms, she wore no cloak.

"Sh!" said Melissa indignantly. She blushed a little under the men's admiring stares and put up a hand to tuck a strand of hair beneath the golden ribbon around it.

The captain of the ten, pushing roughly forward to the front of his men, said something loudly in his own language.

"Sh!" hissed Melissa again, pointing with a gesture of

dismissal in the direction from which they had come.

The captain hesitated. He understood well that Melissa was of a rank he should not meddle with. But it was common knowledge in the army that Miltiades had tried to betray them on the Danube. It was said that the Great King had sworn revenge. In that case, it need not matter much if his womenkind were roughly handled. This one was wearing gold enough to enrich himself and all his ten. He lurched against her and snatched at one of the gold clasps she was wearing.

He ripped it off, and the loose garment fell away from her shoulder. But Melissa did not trouble herself about how she looked. With a furious movement, she wrenched the knife from her girdle and stabbed him between the neck and shoulder, where the scales of his fishlike armor did not protect him. He gave a gurgling cry and collapsed at her feet, his blood spurting down the side of her white robe.

His ten started forward, spears raised. The guards, though taken aback by the sudden catastrophe, would not see their mistress hacked to pieces. Leaping to the rescue, they interposed their shields and drove back the intruders.

At the clash of arms, other soldiers ran in. Only the narrowness of the court prevented the guards from being massacred. They retreated to a little portico which covered the entrance to Melissa's private room. Here they prepared to fight to the death, while Melissa watched them, rocking her baby in her arms.

"Fire! Fire!" In the confusion someone upset a brazier on which Melissa had been brewing her potions. A jar of oil went down with a crash. Smoke also came seeping in from other parts of the palace where soldiers, unable to get at the battle itself, had vented their wrath. In consequence, those trying to enter the palace were soon opposed by those trying to get out. The struggle spread to the street, where no one was perfectly certain whether they were fighting against men or a conflagration.

While this uproar was starting at the palace, Metiochos had been making a friend. Some of the cavalry had ridden in behind Darius, and a young man had asked in tolerable Greek where to hitch their horses. Metiochos had pointed to a corner of the market which he had ordered cleared. The young man had nodded approval and had relinquished his horse to a servant. At that moment a soldier had coolly emerged from the temple of Athene with a silver cup at his belt.

The young man summoned him. The soldier looked anxious to give up his plunder and slink away. He had, however, to listen to a blistering tirade which was too idiomatic for Metiochos to understand. Presently the young man explained.

"I have told him that he will stand guard over this temple, he and the rest of his ten. I will also post others. If anything is missing, he will pay with his head. If not, his ten will assuredly teach him that other men's gods are to be respected in future."

Metiochos thanked him in halting Aramaic. "May I know your name?"

"I am Gergis, son of Ariazos," said the young man proudly. "My mother is the eldest sister of the King. You will be that son of Miltiades about whom the King has spoken."

Metiochos's heart gave a distinct thump. It had not occurred to him that the King would mention hm. Nor was he sure that he was glad of the distinction. On the other hand, he liked the look of Gergis, who was lean and hawk-like, and whose magnificent armor was battered by fierce fighting. They smiled at each other. Gergis posted his guards around the temple with an air of crisp command.

Greeks came panting up to Metiochos. "Fire in the palace! Fighting inside it!" Metiochos had only to turn his head, for the palace abutted on the square, though the bustle around the temple had prevented him from seeing the trouble sooner. Smoke was rising from what he at once perceived was the women's court. He grasped his new friend by the arm. "The Princess is inside there nursing her child!"

Gergis took a quick look. The milling crowd around the entrance was attracting men from all over the market-place. By now the way in was blocked to anything except a cavalry charge.

"Is there another door?"

Metiochos was thinking rapidly. The palace, which dated from earlier, troubled times, was really a stronghold. It had no outer windows or side doors, and the walls around were massive. On the other hand, they were only one story high.

"Get me some men to hoist me up," he said. "I'm going over."

Gergis glanced at him. Metiochos was wearing a long

knife, but he had no armor. "I'll come with you." He threw down his bow and quiver and began to strip off his armored tunic, which was too clumsy for dropping off ten-foot walls.

"Tell your men to make ladders and follow," Metiochos said. "Our rope is all in use, but they can knot cloaks or pile up the market booths. We shall need men in armor."

He raced toward the wall of the women's court which, being at the back, was nearly deserted. Looking around with his imperious air, Gergis shouted. Two men who were captains of hundreds came running over.

When he joined Metiochos, the boy had already collected half a dozen men by the wall. One was mounted on another's shoulders. Metiochos was scrambling onto the top of the heap.

He was up and peering into the smoke which hung over the courtyard. The wool for the looms had caught, and beside it lay the main storeroom of the house. Below him the fight was still going on. Many people had fled the fire, but those who had their captain to avenge were battling with the guard.

Metiochos did not think he could make a leap onto the hard sand of the court without breaking a leg. Unluckily, the top of the wall offered no handhold for a drop. He moved swiftly onto the roof of the women's rooms, peered over, and launched himself onto a soldier below who, taken by surprise, lost shield and spear. They went rolling over, and Metiochos tried to beat the man's head against a stone. His helmet protected him. In another

moment the boy was dashed against the ground so hard
the breath went out of him. His arms, which had been
clinging to his opponent's back, relaxed. The soldier
shook himself free and started to turn. Metiochos moved,
too; but he was lying on his knife and could not draw it in
a hurry. In brute strength he was no match for this man.

Strong hands were seeking his throat. He twisted away
from them and kicked. He might as well have kicked a
wall. A knee jabbed into his stomach and doubled him
up, retching.

Melissa, who had snatched up a jar, sent it whizzing
with savage, accurate aim. It hit the soldier on the back
of his leather helmet and smashed into fragments, knock-
ing him over. But apparently his head was too hard to
be much damaged. He grunted and raised himself. Metiochos at last had drawn his knife.

With a wild yell, Gergis descended from the wall in the
same fashion that Metiochos had done. But the soldier on
whom he dropped had no sooner twisted about to face
his antagonist than he gave a horrified shout and tried to
roll away. Gergis, who had jumped with knife in hand,
stabbed hard. Another soldier whirled around, spear
raised, to help his comrade. He, too, perceived that the
dress of Gergis was that of no common man. He turned
and fled. Gergis, meanwhile, gathering his legs beneath
him, launched himself from behind on that enormous soldier whom Metiochos so far had failed to damage.

Other people were scrambling over the wall on make-
shift ladders. The smoke, which had been blowing away

from that side of the court, came suddenly pouring over everyone in a suffocating cloud. Coughing and choking, men lowered their arms to gasp for breath.

Melissa ran out of the smoke-filled room carrying her child. Metiochos caught her. He and Gergis had killed their bull-like enemy. Both knives were red. "This way!" He guided her out of the smoke. "I thank you for saving my life."

Melissa gave one of her old confiding smiles. "I owed you that." She thrust her son into his arms. "I cannot hold him if I have to mount this ladder. Carry him for me!" Suddenly they two were friends again. Melissa steadied herself as she started to mount with a hand on his shoulder. He had always loved her, he thought fleetingly, and he always would. Was she not the first woman who had ever been kind to him? He followed with caution.

The Great King, in his chariot still, was asking questions outside and giving orders. He took no notice of Melissa, but a Persian who spoke some Greek came bustling up to her. He had found quarters for her among the tents, together with refreshments, clothes, attendants, and a doctor. The King had spoken.

In what seemed less than a moment, Melissa had gone. The crowd around the palace had melted away. Regular detachments were moving in to beat out the fire or save the contents of the palace. People were scurrying about under the eye of the King, who was evidently angry.

There was nothing for Metiochos to do. He leaned against the wall and felt gingerly at his stomach, which was hideously sore. But after a moment he had an insistent, uncomfortable thought that the Great King was looking at him. Glancing timidly in the King's direction, he found this was so. With a tiny lift of the head and raising of the eyebrows, the King beckoned.

Metiochos drew near, but the King did not address him. He was pouring out commands, not about the palace, but concerning the embarkation of his troops, which was not going as rapidly as he expected. Evidently the Great King knew precisely how many camels he had, how many donkeys, what proportion of the baggage of his troops was needed for each hundred crossing the straits. He had discovered how many boats and rafts there were, how many had been fitted up for animals, where they were docking, and what improvements could be made at a moment's notice. Men came and went like bees from a hive. The only ones idle were the Persian nobles who stood by him and who, from their anxious expressions, might be thought to be those whose arrangements had displeased him. Presently he began to dismiss these also with curt commands. It could then be noticed that each took with him a number of men, so that the bustle about the King began to diminish. Eventually there was no one coming with a report or waiting for orders. Darius, with the air of one who when he is working wastes no moments, put out a broad hand to grip his chariot rail and turned on Metiochos.

"There is a slave called Cleon," said the King unexpectedly, "who caused my bridge to be broken and my cities to rise in rebellion against me. I will put out the eyes of this Cleon and cut off his nose and ears. I will nail him up alive by the city gate of Sestos as a warning to other slaves. Where is he?"

The King had not raised his voice in anger. He gave the impression that he was stating a fact, not making a threat. Metiochos's blood ran slightly cold.

"Cleon fled from us to Byzantium, O King," he said, inwardly anxious lest he be not believed. "That town was already in rebellion. Whether he remained there or took ship I have not heard."

The King took his time to decide whether he would accept this statement; but after an agonizing moment, he gave his little nod.

"Your ships are in good order," he said. "This has been well done. Men shall be punished for the burning of your palace. What will you have in return? It is not fitting that Sestos should fare less well at my hands than Byzantium."

Metiochos licked his lips. The granaries of Sestos, thanks mainly to Miltiades's silver, were full enough. But there was unrest and would be more until the town had recovered from the capricious blows of a war which had ruined many. Compensation would merely offer more to quarrel about.

"O King of Many," he said as boldly as he dared, "is not a strong ruler the greatest of blessings? Forgive Miltiades, O King, and let him return for the sake of Sestos."

The King's black brows came down in a frown and he made no answer. For a long moment Metiochos had the uncanny impression that he knew what the Great King was thinking. It was almost as though the personality of Darius was so powerful that his very thoughts asserted themselves. The King was saying to himself, "This Miltiades will always give trouble to me, but the boy has sense. I can use him."

"So be it," he said at last. "Miltiades may return. But never ask another favor."

He gestured at those who stood by his horses' heads, and the chariot moved on. Metiochos watched in an awe that amounted to fear. This king was always looking for good servants. He thought he had found one in a foreign-speaking boy from a little town three long months' journey from Persia. It was frightening. For Metiochos did not want to serve the King.

A Woman's Choice

METIOCHOS did not catch sight of Cleon again until some years later when they met strolling through the marketplace at Athens. Their last memories had not been pleasant ones, but Cleon came forward with an eagerness which banished the past. "How tall you've grown!" he exclaimed admiringly. "Well met again! Since the Athenians drove Hippias into exile, everyone comes to Athens to have a taste of her democracy."

Metiochos laughed. He was not pleased by the meeting because trouble, which he sought to avoid, dogged Cleon's footsteps. All the same, he owed him a good deal and wished to be pleasant. "You're going gray," he remarked, "but you look well as ever. What are you doing?"

"Sowing seed."

This was the old Cleon in mischief. Metiochos sighed. The abortive revolutions which Cleon had fomented inside the Greek cities of the coast had been put down in blood. Since then, hatred of tyrants had burned more fiercely than ever beneath the surface. Besides, the brilliant energy of the new Athenian democracy was showing people what they might do for themselves if freed from the Persian. The situation was ominous enough without Cleon's assistance.

"Miltiades, I hear," Cleon persisted, "bides his time. They tell me he is not so beloved as he used to be."

Again Metiochos could find no answer. It was true that the Chersonese had lost vitality with its independence. People talked of the good old days, blaming Miltiades for a situation which he resented more than anyone else. He was not hated yet, but it was hard to keep up the pretense that he alone among tyrants was a popular ruler.

"I'm here about my marriage," Metiochos said lightly, changing the subject. "To the sister of Conon. You remember Conon?"

"Is she pretty?"

He laughed. "I caught a glimpse of her at Athene's festival, where she was carrying a basket of fruit in the procession. Yes, she is pretty — and young, and shy, and well brought up. It is only a betrothal for the next year or two. But my father wished it settled." He wanted Cleon to understand he had no share in the Chersonese. His inheritance was the Athenian property. His father was anxious to make this clear for the sake of Melissa and Cimon, even if the suitable girl was too young for marriage.

Cleon looked him full in the eye. "So you are to settle down in Marathon, breed horses, and win the chariot race at Olympia!" He smiled scornfully. "You're restless as the sea! I don't believe it."

Faint color seeped into Metiochos's brown cheeks, which were close shaven, following the latest fashion. He had found no niche in Athens, where people considered him too young to be entrusted with responsibility. He had himself thought of horse-breeding, but secretly it bored him.

"Better put off that pretty little girl," Cleon warned him. "There's a great war coming."

"A woman-hater still!" Metiochos tried to be flippant.

"A soothsayer once told me," said Cleon darkly, "that a woman should betray me! I never gave one a chance!"

Metiochos laughed. He had managed to sidetrack the conversation, and deliberately he kept it off the coming war. He did not want to be drawn into a conspiracy. But he did put off his marriage with excuses while he tried to settle into the new Athens. There was plenty going on, but he could not fit himself into subordinate roles under amateur leaders.

The war which Cleon had predicted broke out in Miletos and spread along the coast like fire in a high wind. Cities and islands cast out their tyrants and defied the Persian. There was wild jubilation and fine talk of unity. The campaign on the Danube had taught the cities their strength when they acted together. Even the Athenians, flattered by the appearance of so many democracies, sent twenty ships to fight for the new freedom.

"Twenty ships!" growled Cleon, seizing a chance to pour out his anger to Metiochos, who was waiting beside the docks to embark. "What use is this token force against the Persian?"

Privately Metiochos agreed, but he pointed out to Cleon that the unity of the rebels had not spread to the mainland. The Athenians had enemies at their own door who would take instant advantage if their whole war fleet was sent to Asia Minor. But an initial success might draw the mainland in.

So Metiochos said, and so indeed he thought as he embarked in full armor, carrying his rations. A few weeks later, he was back in Athens furiously angry. Instead of joining a combined fleet, the Athenian general had lent himself to a senseless scheme of raiding Sardis, the Persian governor's headquarters. Sardis, being in the interior, could not be held. It was not even a Greek city and had no desire to be connected with the rebellion on the coast.

Metiochos had to admit the expedition had been successful up to a point. The Athenians understood this sort of warfare, since they were accustomed to raiding or being raided by their neighbors. But because they had not any object but plunder, they scattered through Sardis as soon as they got inside. Their enemies coalesced. In the struggle which followed, Sardis was set afire. It burned furiously. The Athenians retreated, not much richer than they had come, but pleased with themselves for giving the Persians something to think about. They had simply no conception of the riders who were fanning out through the countryside calling up forces from towns not too far away. Since they had marched all night and fought a good deal of the day, they did not hurry back to the coast.

The consequences, Metiochos felt, could have been foreseen by anybody with a slight knowledge of war. They were caught before they could embark. They had to fight a battle in a confined space which gave little room for maneuver and where they offered a mass target to Persian archers. It was true that the Athenians and the Milesians who were with them had fought well. But the idiocy of their commanders had given them no chance. They had lost many and had been lucky to get off at all, abandoning their wounded. The Athenian commander had promptly sailed for home, and it was evident that the people as a whole felt he had shown good judgment. They wanted no part of a war in which they got hard knocks.

Metiochos, too, would have been glad to be finished with the war. From the little he had seen of the Milesians, he had no hope of their success. But wars are not easily put aside at will. In the Chersonese, Miltiades had wasted no moment in throwing over his allegiance. Had he failed to do so, his subjects would have driven him out. As it was, he remained almost the only tyrant still in power. But

Miltiades, like the Athenians, had enemies at his own door. He could not send his ships to help Miletos as long as the Persians held garrisons on the coast of Thrace and in the northern islands. He would have to fight against these for his very existence. Metiochos could hardly let him do so while enjoying his estates in Attica. If the Athenians refrained from the war, he would have to go back to Sestos.

Sestos looked shabby and small after Athens, but everyone was glad to see him. Even Melissa, reassured by his sojourn in Athens, was grateful for his loyalty. Her golden eyes smiled as she said that she had missed him.

Miltiades was thinner, and there were lines on his forehead. He and Metiochos took some of the islands and aided King Oloros in clearing Persian forces from Thrace. But they did not discuss the course of the war with one another. They understood without words that these small operations, no matter how brilliantly planned, were too late. The North Aegean empire could not be consolidated in wartime. It would fall to pieces as soon as the Greeks were conquered in the south.

Sestos still vibrated with news, and all of it was ominous. There was jealousy between Miletos and her allies. Operations inland proved Greek infantry was no match for Persian cavalry and archers. Miltiades said the men were badly commanded. It seemed likely.

The war dragged on, their little successes in the north punctuated by reverses in the south. Miletos was besieged on the landward side, though it could not be taken as long as the combined fleet kept the port open. The Persians brought up their Phoenician fleet from the Levant. A great naval battle impended. Passing traders said that the contingents of the Greek fleet were quarreling with one another.

The news of the fleet's destruction came to the Chersonese like a distant crash of doom. Miletos was as good as lost. The other cities would fall to the Persian one by one, resisting only out of despair. The Chersonese would not be gathered in until after the great cities, but its turn would come. What would happen to Sestos?

There was a strange, subdued atmosphere in the town that summer and in the winter which followed it. It was not natural that people should lower their voices as they talked or stand in silence looking at Asia across the straits. In the early days of their new independence, the Sestians had reverted to their old zest for local affairs. They cared nothing now. Men openly wept when they heard what had happened to Miletos.

In the early days after the disaster, Miltiades looked like a stricken man. He talked hopefully; but his color betrayed him, as did the graying of his beard. Metiochos went dutifully out with the ships on useless expeditions, concealing a restless boredom with them. Sestos was so petty and this northern war such folly. Athens had spoiled him, though when he was there he had not thought so. He belonged in neither place and had been trapped into defending a cause which he had always known was hopeless.

In the following spring when catastrophe could not be much longer delayed, Miltiades brought the fleet to port in Cardia, which lay on the Aegean Sea across the peninsula from Sestos. He said that the arrangement was convenient for the islands he controlled. But it was also a back-door exit if the Phoenicians should block the straits. He went over to inspect the naval stores in Cardia and promised that he would send a packtrain across from Sestos. He went back to Sestos, taking along with him Metiochos, who had been overseeing the spring training of the crews.

All these moves were apparently casual. There had been minor trouble on the small land frontier at the peninsula's neck, and Miltiades had sent up his guards. The palace in consequence was curiously empty. Metiochos was not invited to comment and did not examine the rooms off the men's court to see who was in them. But he noticed the silence that night. He could never remember the palace with nobody stirring.

He slept uneasily and woke with a start to hear cautious movements.

"Metiochos, I want you." It was Miltiades, speaking in a whisper.

He got up hurriedly and dressed. Miltiades was muffled in a cloak, so he took one also. His feet were bare.

Miltiades led the way to the women's court, in which Metiochos had not set foot since the day he had rescued Melissa. There was a pale flame of lamplight from a stand inside her room. She met them at the doorway, finger on lips. "I gave the women sleeping potions, but be quiet!"

Miltiades brushed past her. Metiochos followed. There were chests in the room, two for clothes and one for silver. Miltiades undid a massive lock and raised a lid. Melissa brought over the tiny lamp and stood behind him. Metiochos caught his breath. He had not imagined his father was so rich. There were gold darics from Persia with the sign of the running archer, representing King Darius. There were silver coins from Athens with Athene's owl. There were coins from Miletos, Samos, Ephesos, all the cities which traded through the straits. There were also daggers, belts, cups, brooches of precious metal, seal rings with beautiful stones. From her clothes chest, Melissa brought out her personal adornments, often barbaric, but glittering with gold.

They piled the treasure on the floor and started to wrap it in pieces of cloth which Melissa fetched from the storeroom, tying the coins in tight little packages, lest they chink. Beside them, the pile of parcels grew while they worked in silence.

Melissa brought stout bags which she must have had her women prepare. They put things in. Each shouldered one, including Melissa. They crept out through the court.

Donkeys were tethered by the entrance with panniers on them. Miltiades went back for another load. They moved off through the sleeping town, across the marketplace, Miltiades leading, and the other two behind.

The warehouse for naval stores was by the docks. The grain in it was stored in leather sacks, more convenient than jars for stowing aboard. In one corner lay a separate heap of these which, as Miltiades told his son in a whisper, were already marked. They slipped their parcels inside, deep down into the grain.

"Remember," Miltiades said, "when you get to Cardia, put all these together. Be sure they are not used. If it were discovered I had moved my treasure out, there would be panic in Sestos. But when we leave, I must have wherewithal to pay the rowers. I'll not have it said that I left my men to starve when we reached Athens."

Metiochos nodded with understanding. Athens was final. If Miltiades thought he could ever return to the Chersonese, he would have gone to Oloros. Melissa, who was standing beside Metiochos, put a tentative hand on his arm. He pressed it reassuringly. But Melissa, he felt sure, would never like Athens. She was a king's daughter and had been a queen. She would not fit easily into democracy.

They took their donkeys trotting back in the dark across the marketplace, every stick and stone of which they knew. There was a farewell in each step; but even while he felt it, Metiochos remembered another dark night when he stood outside the gate at Marathon, sick with sorrow, yet burning to know what lay ahead. Sestos was too petty a place for a man to spend his life in. If he had never come back, he would never have found this out. But in the frustrations of this ill-conceived war, he had lost illusions.

Farewell had to be said again on the following morning when he left with the baggage train for Cardia. From the low hills behind Sestos, Metiochos looked his last on the strait and swallowed a lump in his throat. But the world which lay at his feet was no longer friendly. He turned away.

Not ten days afterwards, a ship of Aegina going north to the Black Sea put in at Sestos. Aegina was a neighbor and enemy of Athens, so that her captains preferred Abydos on the farther shore. But they had with them a passenger whose friends, it seemed, had offered a great sum if he were put ashore outside the King's dominions. Cleon was grayer than ever. His well-worn tunic and shabby brown cloak were quite familiar to many Sestians, but no one called a greeting. People fell away as he walked down from the quayside toward the marketplace, almost as though he had some disease. Cleon did not look at the people. There were deep lines on either side of his mouth as though he had forgotten the quick way he used to smile. His eyes were red-rimmed, and runnels worn by tears ran down from the corners, as they do with very old men.

The ship from Aegina was putting back to sea without a word, unwilling to risk itself in an Athenian town, or possibly anxious to be a long way off when trouble arose. Meanwhile, Miltiades, who had been sitting in council, came out of his palace and into the marketplace, where quiet voices, strangely subdued for Sestians, told him that Cleon had landed. Frowning, he turned towards the quay so that, between an avenue of curious faces, the two met.

Neither man said anything for a moment. Perhaps they remembered the past when they had been friends and were taking in what time had accomplished. Then Miltiades said with a stony face, "You have done us so much harm with your Milesian friends and your rebellion that there is little more you can do. So why have you come?"

Cleon gave the ghost of his old smile. "You'll not believe it, but I might have got clear away. I wanted to warn you. Too many have died on our account already." It could be seen that tears did actually gather in his eyes and make their slow way down the well-worn channels.

"Warn us?" Miltiades retorted with scorn. "Do you think we do not know that the Persian will come to take vengeance?" The lanes of people were pressing closer as newcomers pushed in to miss no word, but all kept silence.

Cleon turned his head and looked about him. "It's always better to have a few hours' warning of disaster. The Phoenician war fleet is sailing for the straits. They'll block the entrance in a day, perhaps in a few hours. There's no way out."

A buzz of talk arose. Miltiades threw up his hand for silence. "Sestians! Our ships are not in the straits but on the Aegean. They are waiting for those who must get away. No need for panic."

He paused and looked slowly around him, scanning the faces turned to his. "We have not served you badly, my family and I. But what good can I do you nailed up in the marketplace for vultures to feed on? If any others dare not remain, let them meet me in the marketplace within the hour, bringing what they can carry or load upon one donkey. Your elders will greet the Phoenicians with news that we have fled. Go to your homes, and do not linger in the marketplace to say farewells, lest these be reported."

The talk broke out again. The crowd drew together and then slowly began to break up. Each man pushed forward to look at Miltiades until he caught his eye. No word was uttered, but in this way the Sestians said good-bye to their lord.

It was noon on the following day when the squadron got off. It had not been possible to march all night, for the terrain was rough. Miltiades hastened as much as he could, but there were over fifty people of all ages to pack on the ships at Cardia besides their possessions, together with the crews of the ships themselves, both rowers and soldiers. Miltiades would not leave a fighting man behind, lest the Persians enslave them when he was gone, to punish rebellion.

Miltiades captained the first ship in the post of danger, giving Metiochos the rear. In the middle he put Melissa and her children, distributing his treasure among the five ships equally, lest one fall into enemy hands with all that he possessed. Meanwhile Cleon, who was waiting with the rest, walked up to Metiochos and said, in a low voice, "Take me!" Metiochos nodded consent. Cleon thought he might be safer with one who did not bear him malice. He had survived while many had died, and he understood how to do so.

Miltiades walked up and down on the quay while people were loading, and he deliberated his course with his son. He might sail down this side of the Chersonese, shoot over to Lemnos, an island which he still controlled, and then past other islands to Athens by the direct route. By doing so, he risked being seen by the fleet sailing up to the straits. He might follow the mainland along the coast of Thrace and down by Greece. But there it was not possible to avoid going ashore. Warships packed their space with fighters and rowers, never attempting to be independent of land. They did not even carry water for over twenty-four hours. Miltiades dared not make landings in northern Greece. The Macedonians, Thessalians, or others might think it safer to lay hands on the loser in this war and use him to buy the favor of the King.

Metiochos turned round to beckon Cleon. The wind stood fair for the islands, but where was the enemy fleet? If they rounded the tip of their own peninsula and met it coming up to block the strait, they were certainly lost. And time had been wasted which had been counted upon.

Cleon thought that they must risk the islands. Macedonia was a certain trap. The oracle of Apollo at Delphi favored the Persians and would excuse an act of treachery. The fear of the Great King was spread all over northern Greece.

Miltiades bit his lip as he considered. "We'll go by the islands!"

They set out along the shore in a careful column, keeping together more out of instinct than from any knowledge that five ships were better than one against a fleet. Miltiades set a slow, steady stroke; and he rested the men at their benches every hour while the wind took them. He was anxious there should be no delay, but strength might yet be needed.

The wind and the spray of the oars, the coast gliding steadily past them were calming to the nerves. Women who had staggered aboard dust-covered and in tears had managed mysteriously to straighten their garments. Old men accepted a measure of water and wine doled out with care, for liquids must be reserved for the rowers. These latter, bronzed and nearly naked, swung steadily to the monotonous chant which set their pace. The twin helmsmen, maneuvering the steering oar, kept the ship in the wake of the others. There was little for Metiochos to do but look more cheerful than he felt. They were approaching the end of the cape in the late afternoon, a bad moment. Miltiades dared not wait till dark, lest the fleet seize the islands and cut him off from them.

Already the Chersonese was receding to the east. Metiochos went up into the prow to see what he could. Suddenly he heard the war gong start in Miltiades's trireme, sounding heavily to give quick time to his rowers over the noises which might distract them in battle. The second ship and the third were following suit. As he swung his own after them, Metiochos saw the enemy off to the east and sailing north, the nearest no more than a mile away, but spread to the horizon. Even as he watched them, he could see them turn and swing to cut him off.

A mile is a long start in a race, even allowing that the Phoenicians must have with them some bigger ships which took two hundred men. But if they turned and fled now, they would be penned against the land. If they went on for the islands, they would have to pursue a slanting course which would bring ships now to their southward in a po-

sition to intercept, or hope to do so. Indeed, if there was
more of the fleet over the horizon, their chances of escape were very meager. It required strong nerves to hold
this course and stronger ones to remember that the rowers
could not be worn out in a single burst. All depended on
the skill with which their strength was husbanded.

Metiochos had his sail trimmed to get the maximum out
of the breeze, which still blew in their favor. He made
his passengers sit down. He concentrated on keeping his
distance from the ship ahead, while yet measuring his
rowers with a calculating eye. Each crew would vary. It
was hardly likely that they would end this race in the close
squadron in which they had begun it.

The central ship, Melissa's, that from Cardia as it happened, was beginning to lose ground. Niceratos, who
captained the one behind it, was not disposed to wait —
and who could blame him?   The two raced neck and
neck. He could see the captains exchanging shouts. Eventually the Cardian fell back again. Metiochos considered. His task was the rearguard, and yet it would be
folly to lose two ships instead of one. Besides, the Cardian
was a good ship. Most probably the captain had slackened his rowers off, and time might prove him wise. The
enemy nearest when they rounded the point were far behind them, spreading out to cut off retreat. Ahead, ships
starting further away were racing to intercept. If ever
Miltiades needed good judgment, it was now. He did not
swerve.

Metiochos was coming up on the Cardian. He could
see Melissa standing by the helmsmen, hair whipped loose

by the wind, with Cimon beside her, clutching her skirt. The captain appeared on the stern and made a trumpet out of his hands to bellow something which the wind snatched away. Metiochos leaped onto the gangway and ran to the prow. The voice of the captain came faintly over the intervening waves. "Give us water!"

Metiochos was overwhelmed with seething fury. The first task of a captain was to see his waterskins aboard. If in the hurry this had been neglected, or partly so, why had he not announced his need sooner? The fool had been afraid to delay. He had simply hoped to get clear off without exposing his men to a chase under the blazing sun. He had lost his gamble.

"Let him go, let him go," growled Cleon, taking him by the elbow. "Whose fault is it but his own if he is captured? Niceratos refused him." He pointed to the ship ahead, now racing after the others.

"Let me think," Metiochos snapped, pushing Cleon aside. Melissa's little girl, whom he had always loved, caught sight of him and lifted a hand to wave. He answered mechanically, peering ahead. Miltiades was going to get away, and he could also. He had his men to think of. On the other hand, if there was time to save the Cardian, he had to think of those men, too — and of Melissa. It was not for Cleon to tell him what to do. It would be a near thing, but his men were well trained; and he thought there was a chance.

"Get out ten skins of water," he snapped, "and hold them ready." He turned to yell to the Cardian, thankful that the wind was in his favor, since he had not time to repeat himself. "We're coming alongside!"

It took ten seconds to thrust those skins aboard, ten precious seconds. But many minutes were wasted slowing down, shipping and unshipping oars, drawing free, and settling once more into their pace. There was no question of waiting for the Cardian now or even of husbanding strength. Metiochos stood by the man at the gong and made him quicken the rowers. He could see sweat running in rivulets down their chests, and he set the soldiers he had with him to wiping them with wet cloths as they swung forward, which was not easy because of the crowding of the men in their benches. His passengers were too clumsy for this work, but he collected them, men and women alike, and made them pitch the cargo overboard. A fifth of Miltiades's treasure, everything but the water and wine and a few sacks of corn went over the side. Very slowly they crept up on Miltiades, a half mile ahead. The Cardian came straggling after.

Metiochos felt a glow of pride in his crew, on whose training he had worked hard himself. Few could have accomplished so much, and yet the time lost had been crucial. Luckily they had not the strength to spare to look over their shoulders, because unless they were fortunate, they would not get away.

A single Phoenician was racing across their path. It must have happened to be in the best position and to have had the best-trained crew. Behind it, but at some distance yet, a bunch of half a dozen were straining to catch up. If the foremost used her battle ram, she must either damage her opponent or delay him long enough to make capture certain. Metiochos would have sheered off to the west, but his men were too exhausted for another endless chase. There were still two hours till dark.

The Phoenician actually crossed their course and turned straight down toward them. Metiochos made signals to the Cardian to take her in the side as he drove forward. The maneuver would be certain death to the Phoenician, rammed from two directions at once. Not improbably he might not think the capture worth such sacrifice. He might sheer off.

Metiochos let the Cardian draw level and saw the captain gesture with understanding of what he ought to do. The Cardian's helmsmen flung their weight on the steering oar to bring her round. Melissa, still standing in the stern, put out her hand with a gesture as though demanding something of the captain. Metiochos had no time to think of her. He steadied his steersman with anxious nicety, drawing the Phoenician sideways to the Cardian's onrush, his eyes ahead.

A hand fell on his arm, gripping tight. Cleon shouted in his ear over the noise of the gong, "The Cardian's turning!"

Metiochos shook him off. This was no moment in which to explain naval maneuvers. Only after an instant did he realize that Cleon was no tyro at this game.

"She's saving herself," howled Cleon, "leaving us to be taken!"

Metiochos took his eyes off the Phoenician with a start.

The Cardian was drawing rapidly away. Melissa still stood in the stern looking backward at him. Already she was too far off for him to see her expression, but Cleon at least had no doubt that this was her work.

"Curse her!" he said with a bitter vehemence which conveyed itself even over the savage beating of the gong. "Betrayed by a woman whom I did not even trust! Betrayed at last!"

"She has her son with her." Metiochos saw death bearing down on them fast, and it was too late to blame Melissa. "Steady on your course," he growled to the helmsmen. He and the Phoenician were rushing together like two bulls, head on.

"I'll not die in torment to amuse the King. Not I!" Cleon put his hands on the gunwale and clambered half over, clumsy in his haste, to balance over the sea. "She'll give way to the west," he yelled, "and try to pen you against those coming up. Swerve east, and you'll slip past her!"

It seemed most probable. Why should the Phoenician shatter his bows against their ram when all he needed was to pass close alongside, breaking oars? Of course he would swerve at the last moment, allowing no time for countermeasures. But it was true that two could play at that game. If they could manage to pass without hitting at all — and such things had been done — they might get away.

"Stand ready to swerve sharply," he yelled to the helmsman. "Ready . . ." Fifty yards between them. Only one more stroke! His eye fell on the rowers, coming gasping to their feet for the hard pull. In a sea of faces he picked out one whose head was rolling backwards. There was blood running from that man's open mouth as though he had bitten his lip but had not time to notice. Nor had Metiochos time either. "Turn!"

The ship heeled violently. The gong gave a single thunderous crash and was silent. The rowers, trained in the maneuver, brought their oars clear forward against the side of the ship and leaned back waiting while the Phoenician slid past at a rush, vainly trying to twist into their side. The soldiers, who had taken up positions on the gangway, yelled in derision.

They were passing. They were past. "Now!" Metiochos shouted. The gong crashed out. The men swung to their feet, pulling back their oars for the stroke which would take them out into clear water after Miltiades to freedom. At that moment, Metiochos saw that one face again, blood still dripping off the chin. It came up lolling, seemed to slide quite gently sideways, and slipped down between the benches out of sight. The oar went trailing loose, and overside a crack proclaimed another oar had caught in it.

Metiochos leaped for the vacant oar, but even as he did so, he knew it was no use. One tangle at a moment such as this, and all was over. Cleon knew it too. He pushed himself gently outward and dropped into the sea. Pursuers came swooping out of the east to seize their prey.

Spoils of War

Boubares the Persian was a young man whose powerful connections had brought him the command of one of the convoys which were carrying spoils from captured cities into Persia. Local governors and generals took their share, granting prizes to any who deserved them. But a proportion of the silver and gold, the best of the fine robes and precious ointments, the most beautiful cups and jewels were sent to the Great King in Susa, that his splendor might be increased by every conquest. Along with such treasures went the cream of the captives, ringleaders of rebellion for the King to punish, or handsome young men and pretty girls to be slaves in his household.

The convoy consisted of a train of laden donkeys, a few hundred guards, and fifty prisoners. It was Boubares's first independent command, and he was in excellent spirits when he marched his soldiers down to the governor's prison, where the captives were having their fetters struck off in the courtyard.

The prisoners were an emaciated group, filthy and ragged, unhealthily white from close confinement, some of them with festering sores from their chains on wrists and ankles. Boubares noted that he would need some extra donkeys, not out of compassion for these slaves, but because it was his duty to see that too many did not die on the road. For the same reason, he saw to it that a cloak and sandals were issued to each man. They were going to march upward of twenty miles a day for three months. Camping in the open, they would be exposed to rain or to cold night dews in the uplands.

Such precautions were essentially sound; but for the sake of example, Boubares would not mount his prisoners until they collapsed by the road. It was wiser to have them driven by sticks until he discovered who could walk and who could not. From the look of them he did not imagine that any would walk far.

Cursing the crowded conditions of the jail, Boubares set his own horse at a slow pace and committed the pack-train to the charge of one of the captains of his hundreds.

Before they as much as got into the suburbs, this began
to draw ahead, splitting the convoy into halves. The
straggling of the prisoners' column had commenced, even
before the road got steep and stony.

All too soon, they came to a dead stop. Three of the
prisoners had fallen in their tracks and could not get up.
One of these was discovered to be dead already. This
would never do. Impatiently Boubares ran his eyes across
the group, trying to make up his mind how many must
ride. He had to take the dignity of his soldiers into con-
sideration. They would not like it if they marched on
foot themselves while all the prisoners were mounted.

A pair of dark eyes met his own, looking out of a face
which seemed all angles, hardly softened by a two-inch
growth of uncut beard. "The men are thirsty," said the
prisoner in passable Aramaic, "and they have had nothing to eat since yesterday noon."

Boubares relieved his feelings by abusing his guards.
Why had not the captain of the hundred seen that his
charges were fed? The responsibility had been that of the
prison, he knew; but his bluster was intended to conceal
the fact that the prisoners controlled the pace of his convoy.

He had another purpose in mind also, as he thought
grimly when the captives had been refreshed and the column restarted. He could trust the captain to take his revenge on the prisoner who had brought on him a public
reprimand. It was well that he should do so. Boubares
wanted no leadership among these slaves. Deliberately
he turned his back, urging his horse forward as though to

overtake the front of the column. Behind him, he heard the crack of a blow and felt half angry that the captain could not wait till he was out of earshot.

Glancing back, he saw they had halted again. The prisoner had collapsed, and soldiers were trying to kick him to his feet; but he was quite unconscious.

The captain was nervous now, as well he might be. "I laid my stick once across his back, and he fell like a log."

Boubares glared at him in fury, but before he could give further vent to his feelings, someone in the midst of the huddle of prisoners called out distinctly, but with a quick nervousness, "Fools! Look at his back!"

"Who said that?" Boubares and the captain both rounded on the prisoners with threatening gestures. They huddled in silence. If they had been in better condition, it would have been easy to beat an answer out of them. As it was, Boubares had to swallow his pride and tell his soldiers they had better look the prisoner over.

He expected to see marks of a beating, but even so, when the back was bared, he caught his breath. It was raw from shoulders to waist, only half scarred over. It must have been agony at every movement. Here was one prisoner who could neither walk nor ride. He would have to be carried. How he had managed to stay on his feet through the streets of the town, Boubares could not imagine.

They brought him to his senses at last. Even the guards perceived he could not march with the rest. They made him a stretcher between a couple of spears after a fashion which they used for their own wounded. They moved on slowly.

Boubares, riding now at the rear, felt considerably sobered. The glamor of presenting gorgeous offerings to the Great King was three months off. In the meantime, he was going to have to play jailer to valuable prisoners who could not be herded like cattle. As they recovered their strength, they might think of escape. To be sure, they would not know the native languages; and no one anywhere would give them refuge. Generally speaking, they would be better off as slaves of the King than as hunted outlaws. But it alarmed him to see that they already had a leader. Boubares was too acute to miss the significance of that frightened, "Look at his back!" Someone had risked a beating for this man, and none of his fellows had curried favor with the guards by giving him away.

His thoughts turned to the prisoner whom they carried. Despite what he had already suffered, that man had not been frightened when he had spoken out. It was indeed for that very reason that Boubares had left him to the captain's mercies. Boubares would have thought himself softheaded if he had wasted pity on prisoners of war. But he could perceive that such a man was dangerous.

Who was this prisoner? How desperate was he? What was his background? The fortunes of the convoy might well depend on answers to such questions. Boubares sent a messenger up the line to find out the prisoner's name. "Son of Miltiades," came back the answer.

Boubares nodded, pressing his lips together as he made inward resolutions to be always on his guard. The son of Miltiades was the prisoner who above all others must be delivered. The Great King had torments ready for Miltiades and had given orders that he should not be allowed to escape. This son of his was sent to turn away the King's wrath by receiving the fate prepared for his father. Doubtless the young man knew what was in store and would be desperate enough to take any risk.

They wound through Lydia and into the uplands. Every eighteen or twenty miles there was a way station on the royal road. Here a string of post horses was kept for the King's messengers, who rode in relay fashion from end to end of his vast kingdom. Here also customs were levied, and other travelers were examined and reported upon. The local governor kept check on all who moved along the King's highway.

After a week, Boubares decreed that the prisoner need not be carried any longer. Let his fellow slaves help him along. Their efforts to do so convinced Boubares again that this man was their leader.

Beyond the highland plateau came the hills. It was late summer as the convoy moved up one side and down the other, past dried streambeds and dusty villages whose very goats bleated for water. On one afternoon when they were trudging along in weary silence through this desert, the prisoner lifted up his voice in a rollicking tune. Even the trampling of the guards fell into its rhythm. A week earlier the soldiers would have shut him up with blows, but — there was no doubt about it — captors and captives were getting used to each other. Boubares, watchful though he still was, decided the prisoner either did not know or had for the moment forgotten that he was traveling toward a death in torment.

By the time they made their second crossing of the Halys, as it curved back along itself, they were passing into the Cilician mountains, which lay across their path in a series of ridges. By this time Metiochos would sing, when he had breath, in Aramaic as well as Greek, improvising rude verses which sufficed to attract a chuckle. Most of the guards had not used their sticks in a week. Where the road was rough and overladen donkeys must be lightened, the prisoners took the burdens without being ordered.

When evening came, the captives huddled around their own campfire, cooked the food handed to them, and never strayed outside their given limits. They sat around their chosen leader and listened to him. Boubares sent the captain of the hundred over one evening to demand what the prisoner was telling them. Without hesitation, he translated into Aramaic a fable about a wolf and a flock of sheep. It was received with delight. A storyteller was a rare prize for the men. Each night thereafter, Metiochos told another fable about a fox, crow, lion, donkey, or other creature, speaking first in one language, then in the other. Guards and prisoners would sit side by side, almost on friendly terms, to listen to him.

By imperceptible degrees, Boubares discovered that his first command had slipped out of his hand. He still gave orders, and they were executed. In general, however, everyone waited for the movements of a dark young man beneath whose gaiety Boubares still suspected hidden purpose. But there was no fault to be found with the prisoner's demeanor. He neither met Boubares's gaze nor attempted to charm him. He merely came between him and the men.

It was a relief, Boubares felt, to drop down from the mountains onto the undulating plain which led to the Euphrates. They were really in the East by now. These Greeks would never consider escape in a land so alien. But what other plan did Miltiades's son have in his mind?

The Euphrates is a rushing river which tears out of the Armenian mountains and rolls headlong south toward the Red Sea. It was now autumn, but the rains had not come yet. At the usual passage, the stream was no more than knee-deep, presenting no problems to the men. The donkeys, however, though surefooted in the hills, disliked the current and the loose stones they could not see. Because of the treasure he carried, Boubares caused a rope to be stretched across to give the men handhold as they pushed or pulled or goaded their animals over.

All should have been well if Boubares had been willing to expose his favorite horse to these indignities. Choosing to lead it instead, he fell with it as it slipped in midstream. Those who hurried to his rescue were forced to haul him up with arms around his shoulders. Supporting him to the bank, they sat him down to examine his ankle, which was already swelling.

There was a silence while the men respectfully waited for Boubares to tell them what he would do. At his orders, they set him on his horse and continued their march. Pain was intended to be borne. Boubares rode for the rest of that day, his olive complexion a whitish-green under his tan. The whole foot was swollen, so that he took his sandal off, while the movement of the horse against his swinging leg was agonizing.

At the end of the day he was in too much pain to feel hungry and sat gloomily sipping wine with his leg stretched before him. They were moving east towards the crossing of the Tigris. There would be no doctors of any skill until they turned south. Besides, Boubares, a young man who had never been ill, had little faith in doctor's magic. Surely a demon who had seized on his foot in the upper Euphrates would not be acquainted with the local incantations of Media.

He saw Metiochos approaching, and he frowned. It pleased him to keep the slave standing in front of him and waiting for his permission to speak. But presently his temper got the better of him, and he snapped angrily, "Who gave you leave to move about as you wish? Get back with the prisoners!"

"It was the captain of the hundred," Metiochos said. "My cousin Hippias, who used to be tyrant of Athens, had a doctor who was famous through all Greece. I have seen him treat such a leg, and I remember what he did."

There was nothing disrespectful in the manner of the dark young prisoner, and it was true that the Great King himself would have none but Greek doctors, whose methods were different from those practiced in Media.

Boubares bit his lip. He actually wondered whether the

demon in his leg and the young man before him were acquainted. Was his accident part of the prisoner's plan? Was he a magician? It seemed likely when one considered the effect he had on the convoy. But while Boubares hesitated, Metiochos beckoned to a couple of soldiers, who obeyed his orders just as though he were an officer over them. Carefully they propped the injured leg in an armload of hay, while Metiochos dipped a cloth into a jar of cold water and gently applied it.

Relief was great, and when the inflammation had warmed the cloth, Metiochos dipped it again. He made no incantations, and he did not look at Boubares. He sat quietly as the stars came out in the sky, simply wetting his cloth every fifteen minutes or so and spreading it anew. It was a service which Boubares could have performed for himself, but he said no word of dismissal. Indeed, he said nothing at all. The moon moved down the sky and set. The stars blazed brighter than ever, so that it was never fully dark. Boubares's leg ached too much for sleep. He had propped himself against a tree, occasionally reaching out to take a sip of wine while he listened to the sentries or puzzled wearily about the prisoner before him. At last when the faint smell of dawn was in the air, his curiosity overcame him. He said quietly, not as though to a slave, but as to an equal, "Why did they beat you in the prison?"

Metiochos changed the cooling cloth for the thirtieth time. "I killed a man."

Boubares gave a little start of sheer surprise. "A man? A guard? And you in chains?"

"It taught the rest a lesson," said Metiochos drily. "I knew they dared not put me to death because the Great King desires to see me die."

So he had known all the time! Boubares could hardly believe it. He said wonderingly, "How could you know your fate and not be afraid?"

"Do you think me a fool?" queried Metiochos curtly. "I am afraid. But I enjoy life while I can. Lamentations will not put off the day of our arrival."

"You are a brave man."

"Such men are not all Persians."

Boubares digested this remark in silence. Metiochos put a gentle hand on his leg and said, "It is growing cooler; but if you ride tomorrow, it will get worse."

"You are an impertinent slave!" Boubares resented dictation.

"Unless you wish to be lame for life," retorted Metiochos unmoved, "you will camp for a week." After a minute he added in the same unemotional tone, "I am trying, as you will readily see, to put off our arrival."

Boubares laughed, as he was meant to do; but he made no answer. He was perceiving that he took orders from this man as well as the rest. He did not like it.

Metiochos went on with his task until the dawn came up, when he told the Persian that he would return when the sun was past the zenith, and that meanwhile he should keep his leg propped without trying to move it. Boubares grunted, still angry at being told what to do. Metiochos removed himself in silent haste to the prisoners' quarters.

"Well, did he speak?" demanded one of these in Greek.

"A little." Metiochos was pale and hollow-eyed. "Now he is angry because I told him not to ride, and he will say nothing."

"You should have led an escape in the mountains. I would have come with you."

"And I."

"And I."

There was a general murmur of agreement.

He sat down, shaking his head wearily. "Must I tell you over again that you are fools? You would have been hunted down with dogs and died in misery. Even slavery will be better."

They did not deny it, but one of them protested, "Not better for you."

Metiochos stretched himself out on his back and shut his eyes. "Let me work on the commander. If the Euphrates had not given me a chance to win him over, I would have made one. But Boubares is a proud man who does not like to think a slave his equal. Give him time."

"There are only five weeks left," the other said.

"Six if we camp for a week."

They did camp for a week, during which Metiochos began to apply hot water instead of cold. The doctor, he explained, had given some reason for this which was connected with the nature and origin of matter; but being no more than a boy at the time, he had not paid attention. He knew nothing about a demon who had entered the leg, but possibly a knowledge of philosophy controlled the spirits. Such was the subject of the only conversation he had with Boubares.

By the time they went on again, the foot could be bandaged. Metiochos improvised a sling from the saddle so
that it should not dangle free while Boubares was riding.
Morning and evening he rubbed the leg from calf to thigh.
They crossed the Tigris and turned south through low
hills. Palm trees appeared along their route. In the
mountains of Cilicia behind them, winter would have set
in now. In these lands it was dry. Presently the road to
Ecbatana, greatest city of Media, divided to the east. They
went on southward. Susa was only a week away.

Metiochos still massaged the leg daily, though he wondered why Boubares permitted him to do what he could
easily by now have done for himself. Was it to humiliate
him? Was the Persian feeding resentment because he
had been forced to listen to a slave? When Metiochos had
first set eyes on Boubares in the courtyard of that prison,
he had promised himself that in the three months' journey he would make the commander see him first as a slave
among other slaves, then as a man, and at last as an equal.
It had seemed easy to work this miracle in three months.
Now he had a week.

Boubares cleared his throat as though there was an obstruction in it. "Is there anyone at Susa whom I might
warn of your coming in time to plead for your life with
the Great King?"

Metiochos let out his breath in a long sigh of relief as
his fingers paused in their unnecessary task. "There is
Gergis, son of Ariazos, nephew of the King."

Boubares shook his head sadly. "Gergis is in Egypt."
So many of the noblemen of the king were seldom at

home. Gergis was garrisoning a town on the Soudanese frontier, controlling a territory larger than Persia.

"I see." Metiochos let his hands drop. It all had been useless. He had brought this man to the point of offering help, and Gergis was in Egypt.

"I shall not see the King myself," Boubares was regretful, "until I make the presentation. Such is the custom. By then it is too late. Once the King gives orders, he will not alter them."

"I see." He met Boubares's eyes with steadiness. "I have had my time, and it is nearly over."

"One meets all sorts of people in Susa," Boubares said. "I will make inquiries to find out if anyone knows you."

Whoever else there might be in Susa, the Great King was not. This was a possibility which had never once occurred to Metiochos. The Great King was hunting and would be away for a week. The prisoners were accommodated in a jail which was really a caravanserai with a stockaded yard for the reception of camels. A small inn, which was attached, was cleared for their guards. The prisoners were given water to wash, and a barber was sent to them. They sat about in the shadow of a dusty fig tree or went to sleep in the shelter that ran like a rough colonnade of poles and thatch around the fence. Low-voiced, they talked about their future, changing the conversation with haste if Metiochos approached. He for his part spent most of his time with the guards, listening to the gossip of Susa.

On the third morning of this tense period of waiting, the captain of the hundred which was on duty came actually running into the yard. Quick, quick! A mighty noble desired to see the son of Miltiades. Without a moment to rally against the shock of this summons, Metiochos was hustled through the inn and into a courtyard which was part of the private quarters of the house.

There was only one man in the court, indeed a great noble if finger rings, earrings, bracelets, and brilliant robes were anything to go by. The stranger's beard, which was a curiously pale brown, was beautifully curled. As he settled his sleeve with a meticulous finger, he perfumed the close air. He said nothing for a moment, but looked Metiochos up and down, parting his pouted lips in a smile which never managed to reach his colorless eyes.

Metiochos blinked. With acute disappointment, he realized that this was no friend of Gergis. Despite his Persian costume, the man was a Greek. So resolutely had Metiochos turned his back on a dead past that it cost him an effort to summon up old faces, none of which possessed the sharp nose and pointed chin he saw before him. The eyes were familiar, however, and that dead hair. He drew himself up, by no means certain whether this man was friend or enemy.

"Well met, cousin."

The other laughed, a braying sound which he remembered well. "Am I then so little changed since we were children?"

"I should never have known you, were it not for your likeness to Hippias." Pisistratos might take that for a compliment if he pleased. "How is your grandfather?"

Pisistratos gave his silly laugh again. "He's hunting."

Metiochos jerked dark eyebrows up. "Impossible! He must be seventy at least."

"He's seventy-five and sits a horse as well as ever. But to tell you the truth, cousin, the King does the hunting and takes his counselors in attendance. You must know Hippias is his chief adviser on the Greeks ever since their rebellion."

Metiochos had not known, but he saw no need to say so. Most of the tyrants of the coastal cities had become involved in the rebellion, preferring to be swept along with their own people. Among them, Histiaeos of Miletos, who used to be counselor to the King, was put to death. Hippias, never a subject of the King, had never rebelled. He depended utterly on the Persian because the Athenians would not receive their hated tyrant back except with a conquering army. It was only natural the King should trust Hippias. Moreover, where his fears and fancies were not concerned, the old man's advice would be sound. He had always been shrewd.

Pisistratos glanced around the court and came a little closer, dropping his voice into a confidential murmur. "Hippias sent me. Does that astonish you, cousin? Your young Persian — must I remember his name — passed him word you were here. Now, Hippias asks nothing of you, I was to tell you, nothing in return for your life — those were his words. But, cousin, you have friends in Athens, as we do. Allied, we might return home and — take our vengeance."

"On whom?"

Pisistratos waved a hand, deprecating such bluntness. "The woman who betrayed you is dead, but were there not others as guilty as she? I name no names — better not — shall we simply say others?"

He was hinting at Miltiades, who was considered by fools to have deserted his son. What good could he have done by turning back? Metiochos, even if his life depended on the matter, would not be drawn into a scheme of vengeance put forward by Hippias, insane on this issue. On the other hand, it would not be wise to say so. He temporized.

"What woman is dead?"

Pisistratos stared at him. "They did not tell you? Oh, of course you have been . . ." He paused tactfully. "What woman? Why, none other than Miltiades's Thracian woman. You know the name I mean. She killed herself."

Metiochos had tried not to think of Melissa because his anger and resentment were so useless. But he could be sorry for her now and even admit she had been fond of him after her fashion. So she had repented what she had done! How like Melissa! Or had Miltiades driven her to suicide by his anger? He hoped not.

"What did I say?" demanded Pisistratos, regarding his dark face in triumph. "You know you have enemies."

"It is more important to your grandfather," Metiochos pointed out, "that I have friends. That is, if I live."

"You'll die of old age, never fear! As far as Greeks are concerned, the King does nothing without a word from

Hippias. In fact," he lowered his voice still further, "the King's persuadable. You have to learn his ways, but Hippias . . ."

"I shall be grateful to him for my life," said Metiochos smoothly.

Should he have said more, he asked himself a thousand times in the long watches of the last nights that he might live. Would what was reported be satisfying to Hippias? Surely the old man must know that family connections in Athens would turn to Miltiades. Only a madman would look for help from him in recovering Athens. Yet Hippias had sent his grandson to sound him out. Luckily the young fool was sure to puff his own importance by suggesting more than his cousin had actually said. No, the anxious question was, did Hippias have the power he imagined? It was not easy to think of the Great King as a persuadable man.

The very same question was occupying the thoughts of Boubares some days later, as he presented his treasures to the King. Every object of value was separately displayed, while Boubares announced what it was and whence it had been taken. Darius, sitting very straight on his throne, was far too lofty to show interest in treasure. At the most he occasionally gave his famous little nod, almost as though he had an involuntary twitch of the head.

Having promised to help Metiochos, Boubares felt that his honor, of which like all Persians he thought a great deal, was involved in succeeding. This morning he had given Metiochos a small, sharp dagger, with which he could kill himself if condemned to the torture. He had refrained from hinting that an inquiry might even mean that he himself would lose his life.

No one save Hippias knew if it had been possible to approach the King with hope of success. At least the old man was present, conspicuous among the King's counselors because of his straggling white beard and Grecian costume. Unlike his grandson, Hippias never dressed like a Persian. In his own eyes, he was tyrant of Athens still; and he bore himself as such on all occasions. Hippias was fidgeting about and craning his neck to peer past other people's shoulders at the procession, in which the prisoners, fitted again with chains, were coming last. He did not look like a man who was calmly certain that his relative's life would be spared.

Metiochos came last of all. Boubares had arranged the matter thus so that the value of the treasure he presented would please Darius first. But under the King's expressionless stare, these hopes wilted. Not even the splendid appearance of the other captives, whom he had reclothed at his own cost, drew a sign of approval.

Boubares cleared his throat, which felt hoarse from speaking. "Metiochos, son of Miltiades, who used to be the tyrant of the Chersonese," he cried, refraining from the catalog of Miltiades's sins against the King which would have been usual.

Metiochos threw himself on the ground before the throne. Hippias moved hurriedly forward into range of the King's eye, making the humble gesture with which those of the inner circle asked permission to speak. Darius ignored him.

"This is a king's son," he said in icy tones. "It is not fitting that he should be brought to me in chains. Who did this thing?"

Consternation of a different sort swept over Boubares. He stammered hastily that the governor . . . that Miltiades had sinned greatly against the King. That the governor imagined . . .

"This is not Miltiades, but his son," Darius interrupted. "Does the governor think me a monster to punish one man for the deeds of another?"

Boubares threw himself down before the King, too, taking refuge in silence.

"Remove his chains," ordered Darius. "I will give him an estate and make him a Persian. Is he not a prince?"

The Persian

THE KINGDOM of Persia lay due south of the Caspian on
the borders of the Red Sea. From between these two seas,
the eastern territory of its empire stretched over Asia in a
wide band, passing through desert and grassy plateaus,
over rolling hills and into highlands, up to the mighty
range of the Himalayas. The people who inhabited these
lands had many names, but in general they were stocky,
olive-skinned men who fought, like the Persians, in tunic

and loose trousers, armed with bow and arrows, shield,
spear, and short sword. For transport of goods they chiefly
used the two-humped camel. They rode donkeys or small
skinny horses, not much bigger than ponies.

Many of these men were nomads, moving over the grazing lands with their sheep. Others were traders, passing
merchandise from market to market, including silk and
spices whose origin lay beyond the edge of the known
world. Still more were settled folk. Their towns lay far
apart but were surrounded by baked brick walls within
which solid houses and even palaces arose. The Persian
governors were connections of Darius himself or great
lords of his kingdom, accustomed to living in state and being served by slaves. Their offices were usually held for
life, so that they reigned in the splendor of subordinate
kings, importing luxuries from every part of Darius's widespread empire.

Splendid these Persians were, but not degenerate. Active men were needed to impose justice on warlike tribes
under native chieftains. Persian governors and their
troops ranged wide. If a prince grew too old for constant
travel, usually he had a son who could be trained for the
succession.

Megabates, who was the governor of Bactria, was an
elderly man who had no children. The King had sent him
several assistants, of whom the latest was Metiochos, the
Greek. This young man had been favored by the King,
who had married him to Phaedime, youngest sister of
Gergis and his own niece. To be sure, the father of Gergis
had been no great lord, since his marriage to the King's

elder sister had dated from before the time that Darius aspired to the throne. Phaedime was the least of all the nephews and nieces of a king who had many wives and children of his own. Notwithstanding, there had been murmurs when the King admitted a man who was no Persian into the circle from which he drew his governors and commanders. Megabates himself had been suspicious of this favorite at first. By now, however, he saw in him the son he might have had if the devil had not laid a curse on him which kept his wives barren.

No such misfortune had beset Phaedime. She was a little woman, but she had borne a large, healthy son; and she was able to smile with her soft dark eyes as her husband bent over to kiss her on the cheek.

"Is he a perfect man?" she murmured in triumph.

He laughed. "Was I to count his fingers and toes? To tell you the truth, he was making such a noise that he frightened me away."

"What will you call him?"

"Megabates."

"Not . . . Militades?"

He took her hand and stroked it. "This is a Persian, little Phaedime. Let him learn to ride fast, shoot straight, and tell the truth like other Persians. When he is older, perhaps we will have him taught Greek . . . yet better not. Since he is my son, he will be restless enough in any case."

Phaedime sighed gently. "I often wonder if you are thinking of your home."

"This is my home. To be sure, the Oxus river is not the

great strait, and the town of Bactra is not Athens. But nor is it Susa, and you do not repine. No, Megabates is my father; the Great King is my master; you are my wife; and I am happy. At the moment I am needed in the council chamber because the chieftain of the Amyrgian Scyths has sent us envoys. Forgive me, but I must not keep them waiting."

He kissed her again and was gone with long strides.

Phaedime shut her eyes because she felt them prickle with tears. Metiochos had so little time to spare! Nor was he brought up in the simple way of boys in Persia. Phaedime loved him, but she was never sure she understood him.

Gergis was not quite certain that he did so either. Gergis arrived a month later, traveling from Persia through Media, Parthia, and across the hills which edge the Oxus valley, following the route along which the King's messengers galloped, bearing his commands or answers to his questions. Gergis came with a convoy of his own servants, making the tedious journey, so he said, for no better reason than that he had not seen his sister for two years. Arriving in Bactra, he showed himself in no hurry to leave. Metiochos was forced by the presence of his guest to spend more time hunting, feasting, sipping wine, and idly chatting than he had done since he first went back to Athens. Manfully he tried to conceal the fact that leisure bored him.

"I was not brought up to live in luxury," he protested when challenged.

"Nor I," said Gergis seriously. "Persian boys are tough."

"I know, I know." Metiochos sounded impatient. "But your fathers had great establishments. You saw our little palace in Sestos. Even that was imposing compared to the Marathon farm or the house in Athens."

"Tell me about them."

Metiochos frowned. "No need. They are not important." He shook his head as if the gesture could toss off memory. "The point is, Miltiades spent his leisure discussing public affairs, not enjoying his riches."

"We might do both."

He smiled. "So Phaedime tells me. In time, I shall learn. When you next see me, I shall have gone to the other extreme and be so fat with good living that I cannot sit a horse."

"Phaedime might be happier then."

Metiochos sighed. "If I could change myself for her sake, you may be sure I would. This miracle, however, is not performed by the god of love."

There seemed no answer to this, and Gergis merely stroked his long, down-sweeping moustaches which mingled with his beard. "What have you for entertainment today?"

"A soothsayer. Do you believe in them?"

"Who does not? A few are charlatans. What do you know of this one?"

Smiling, Metiochos shrugged. "Only that he prophesied the death of a rival. When the man did die, the kin accused him of making his words come true by spells or poison. A great feud hangs on the matter. I have promised that the man shall go unharmed if he can convince me that he does indeed see things which are hidden from others."

Gergis sat up, startled. He had served as an administrator himself and knew how delicate a task it was to settle a blood feud. Yet Metiochos proposed to do so by deciding what he personally thought about this prophet's qualifications. His prestige must be extraordinarily high if he could impose his own verdict. Truly, his brother-in-law, Gergis thought, was a remarkable man!

The prophet was brought in by a couple of soldiers, followed by two clumps of witnesses whose sharp division marked their opposing factions. He was a short man with massive body and head set on small legs. His skin, unusually dark, and his beard jutting forward with the thrust of his chin gave him the appearance of a brigand chief rather than a visionary. He wore at his girdle a handsome, silver-hilted knife with which his fingers kept playing as he scowled on Metiochos, announcing that the trial was unfair. The demon who possessed him did not reveal himself to every man and was not to be ordered up at will. Most probably he would refuse to show his powers.

"Then will he lose a useful servant," retorted Metiochos. "But he need not, unless he pleases, speak to me. Let him speak to my brother."

The prophet moved forward a few steps, the soldiers at his side advancing with him. Boldly he fixed his eyes on Gergis, who looked up and met his stare. There was a short silence. The prophet took his hand from the hilt of his knife and held it up beside his head. Deliberately he moved it across his face and back, still watching Gergis continuously through his spread fingers. He muttered something to himself and moved his hand again. After a moment, he let his arm fall; and then he spoke.

"I see the man who sent you on this journey. He is sitting on a golden chair with feet of silver, holding a golden lily in his hand. There is a canopy over his head, and before him on two stands incense burns. Facing him is an old man in a plain woolen robe. His hair and beard are white and very long. His eyes are pale; his skin is yellow. He leans on a staff, putting the fingers of his right hand to his lips as he speaks about your mission. Other men are present, but I cannot see them well because their thoughts are elsewhere."

There was a reflective pause. Metiochos glanced at his brother thoughtfully. "Well?"

Gergis did not meet his eye. "Surely it has been everywhere rumored that the Great King sent me out. As for the description of his gold and silver throne, is that not famous? And the incense burners also."

"And the old man? The counselor in Greek costume? Is he well known in the East?"

A dull flush mounted Gergis's cheekbones but he answered nonchalantly. "Here in Bactra it is surely known your cousin Hippias is high in the King's favor. You came here two years ago, bringing servants with you who must have known Hippias well. What more natural than that they should boast? This fellow might have heard enough to picture Hippias. It sounded plausible that he should speak to the King of you and me."

"You hear my brother," Metiochos turned to the prophet. "What you have said could have been guesswork. It has not convinced him."

The man scowled. "I speak as my demon bids me."

"Then let him bid you again. Say something to me."

He stared into the prophet's eyes, which were dark and bright, reminding him of moonlight on the sea. He had thought of the sea a thousand times since coming to Bactra, most often of the great strait, but also of the Aegean, studded with islands, or of the distant tip of Sunium, around which the ships must turn to go to Athens. He tried to summon up these pictures now, but could not. He was on a sloping shore with waves breaking over his ankles and pebbles moving beneath his straining feet. He was pushing, pushing with his shoulder, while around him the shadows echoed with whispers which were like shouts a long way off.

"Heave!" cried the prophet suddenly. "Get the boat into the water, fools! Never mind pursuit! Put your shoulders down to it together. Heave!"

Metiochos came back from the beach at Marathon with these sounds ringing in his ears. He passed his hand across his forehead, and it came away wet. "That's what the shadows said to me there," he muttered. "I never heard it so close to me before." He looked at the soldiers guarding the prophet. "You may let this man go free, but before you do so . . ." Deliberately he sought the dark eyes again. "Are you revealing to me the day of my death?"

He shook his massive head, indifferently sulky. "There is a fate laid on you, but I do not know the end."

"Very well." Metiochos turned to the witnesses. "This man's demon has spoken to me. He is a true prophet, and you touch him at your peril."

He watched the soothsayer swagger out, followed by his faction, for whom the others made way with gloomy looks. Not until the soldiers had shepherded these off did he turn to Gergis. "Shall we go riding?"

They rode out together talking idly of indifferent matters. Metiochos made small pretence of being host to Gergis, but dragged him on a tedious round of dusty villages scattered across a drab, flat plain where marmots scuttled into their holes with warning whistles. Here and there lay skeletons of horses or camels, dried and bleached white by the sun. Flies buzzed incessantly. They rode in silence until one or the other aroused himself to start a conversation, which would be politely pursued until it fell dead of sheer exhaustion.

They rested in the heat of the day in the shadow of a humped mound which rose abruptly out of the plain, surmounted by a crumbling earthen wall which indicated that it had been a stronghold once, until presumably its water hole dried up and made it a desert. Their escort produced figs and dates and hunks of bread, washed down by watery wine, lukewarm from the sun. Metiochos, however, would not rest. He started an argument which blossomed into a wager about whether the forest of reeds through which the Oxus ran could be seen from the eastern side of the hilltop. "Come on!" he said, starting to his feet. "Let's settle the matter."

Gergis exchanged pitying smiles with the escort. "Never will your master let anyone rest. A demon possesses him!"

Metiochos forced a laugh. "You think to lie there and get the better of me by the length of your tongue. It will not do. Pay up as the loser or put me in the wrong. Get up, brother!"

He pulled Gergis to his feet and, signing casually to the men to take their ease, strolled with him through the grove and up the hillside, whose sparse shrubs had not long ago been nibbled by sheep. Nothing, however, was still in sight. The hot little breeze brought no sound of distant baaing. Metiochos put the ruined stronghold between himself and his men. On the other side of it he rounded angrily on Gergis. "I take it very ill that you did not tell me the Great King sent you out. Must I learn from a soothsayer that my brother is set to spy on me? I was a fool to trust you."

There was a short pause as Gergis looked around before making an answer. "I followed my orders from the King. Besides, it might have been to your advantage if you had never known."

"Your orders! You would murder your best friend if the King ordered. Slave of a Persian!"

"I do my duty. Who are you to find fault with that, treacherous Greek?"

They glared at each other. Metiochos hit out like a

striking snake. Gergis staggered backwards, dragging the dagger from his belt. "You'll pay for that insult!"

He rushed on Metiochos, who seized his upraised arm. They wrestled for the dagger. Metiochos, who had learned tricks on the exercise ground of his youth, threw Gergis sideways, entangling his legs with his own. He fell upon him. Gergis gave up the dagger and drove his fist hard into Metiochos's stomach.

He hunched himself together with a gasp. Gergis, wriggling from beneath him, fastened on his throat. Where the knife was, they neither of them knew. Metiochos jabbed with his thumb at the Persian's eye, scoring a gash with his nail across the cheek which set blood dripping down into Gergis's beard. His grip did not loosen. Metiochos caught the little finger of one hand and bent it back. There was an audible crack. Gergis's lips parted, showing his teeth in a grimace of pain. His grip relaxed, and Metiochos drew in a hoarse breath of relief. He tensed his muscles for a mighty spring, but Gergis had found the dagger again. The point was hovering six inches from his face.

He watched it warily, seeking to anticipate the second when it would finally move.

"This is folly!" Gergis tossed the weapon from him. It clanged on a stone and slid onto the grass. He got up. "I have told you my orders. Now will you listen while I disobey them?"

Metiochos rose slowly to his feet. He was still angry, but less so than he had been. He managed to nod.

"I was to report on you," said Gergis abruptly. "The

Great King has a task for which he designs you. But because his wish must be an order, he will not speak to you about the matter unless I tell him he may safely trust you."

Metiochos made no comment, merely fixing his eyes on his brother with an expression of grim disapproval.

"You do not like to be spied on." Gergis threw out a hand in a gesture of appeal. "Surely it is better that I, your brother, be given this task than some stranger. You did not really suppose that I would do you harm?"

Considering this, Metiochos admitted, "I did not suppose it. But you must be frank with me."

"I am thinking how best to be so. Do you remember how during the great rebellion the Athenians joined with the Milesians in a raid on Sardis and set the town on fire?"

"Very well. I went with that expedition."

"You never told me." Gergis was astonished.

Metiochos gave a reluctant grin. "It was not convenient to boast of it." He was thinking of the royal banquet he had attended soon after his marriage. It was the King's custom to dine alone behind a curtain; but when eating was over, his guests were admitted into his presence to drink with him. Attendants seated them on cushions scattered over a pavement of colored marble. The royal cupbearer took wine from the hand of the taster and carried it to the King in a golden goblet as a sign that drinking might commence. As he leaned over the King's shoulder with his cup in his hands, he called out loudly for all the audience to hear, "Sire, remember the Athenians!"

The King took his cup without comment and drank

deep. The nobles followed his example. Metiochos was glad that even those who resented his presence hardly knew that he was from Athens as well as from Sestos. He did not like to ask why a king who forgot nothing was publicly reminded about Athens. Later, Hippias told him that on all the great feasts of the King since the burning of Sardis, these words had been spoken.

Hippias had the old trick of smiling with his lips as he spoke, but the few jagged teeth he still possessed had given this grin a wolfish look. "The King is reminding his nobles that he will take vengeance some day," Hippias said. "When he does so, he will need trusted counselors, cousin, to tell him whom to kill. Eh, cousin?" He poked Metiochos in the ribs as though they two shared a joke. But Hippias was in deadly earnest, and Metiochos felt sick.

Thinking of this, he glared at Gergis. "If the King plans vengeance on Athens, let him ask Hippias who is to be killed. I shall never tell him."

"He does not need the information," Gergis countered drily. "The question rather is, who ought to be saved. The Athenians, as you must know, are but the first stage in our conquest of mainland Greece. It is important that the King make friends there as well as enemies."

Metiochos curled his lip in disgust. "Even Hippias must leave some Athenians alive if he wants to be tyrant."

"Hippias is a mad dog. The King needs him because he has his secret friends in Athens. But unless someone controls him, even his supporters will hack him in pieces. Pisistratos is worthless for the task, but you could do it.

This was why the King sent me to you. He wants me to
tell him whether you will be faithful to him, not in
Bactra, but in Athens, where you were born."

Metiochos tried to laugh. "How can you tell that?"

"If you will be so," Gergis said, "the King will grant
you the gift of Miltiades's life."

Metiochos set his teeth, wondering in silence whether
Gergis knew that he had said too much. For all the Great
King's favor, Greek was not Persian. Metiochos owed
his life to the King, but his highest duty must be to his
father. Persians would never feel like that. He would
have to go to Athens, even supposing he did not know
what he would do when he got there.

"Poor Phaedime!" he said, controlling himself to speak
lightly. "She will have to learn Greek after all. I must
get her a teacher."

"You go too fast." Gergis spared an affectionate smile
for Phaedime. "Before she can join you, Greece must be
conquered . . . and then . . . Brother, have you ambitions?"

"Yes . . . No! I am Persian by marriage and nephew
to the King. Megabates trusts me to rule for him in
Bactria. What more can I aspire to?"

Gergis hesitated, on the verge of what he knew was an
indiscretion. But one confidence breeds another. Borne
on by the momentum of what he had already said, he
could not stop himself.

"Would you not wish to be governor of Greece? The
Great King picked you for this service long ago. It was
for this reason that he made you a Persian and a connec-

tion of his own. Greeks need, he thinks, a countryman to rule them."

Metiochos drew in a long breath. He was flattered, astounded, awed, and actually frightened by the long-range plans of the Great King. Gergis, to whom loyalty was the sum of all virtues, was looking imploringly at him, only desiring to be told Metiochos was a faithful servant. He was too straightforward and simple to see that the King would be angry if the instrument he had planned to use was unfit for his purpose. The life of Metiochos as well as Miltiades would hang on what Gergis reported.

Metiochos smiled on Gergis because he had to. Inwardly, he had hard work to repress a shudder. He stood between great peril and a dazzling position whose reality he understood better than the King. As a child in Athens, he had learned how Greeks chafed under military rule. As a boy in Sestos, he had seen how vast Persian plans brought ruin to those of little men. Dwelling on the great strait, he had felt the vibration of a rich and colorful life entirely different from the drabness of Bactria and the splendor of Persia. He had put that life away and could never combine it with the service of the King.

"I am the King's man," his lips said to Gergis.

Gergis beamed. "I always knew it." He put his hand to his cheek and brought it away smeared with blood. He glanced at his finger, which he held at an odd angle. "I should be embarrassed because the men will know we have been fighting. But now nothing matters. All's well."

It was on the tip of Metiochos's tongue to tell him that a story to satisfy the men was easily invented. Only after he opened his mouth to speak did he remember that to the Persian a lie, no matter how white, would be utterly shameful.

"All's well and nothing matters," he agreed, lying himself.

They came back late to Bactra, and Phaedime was angry because while her brother was there, she had been neglected. She sat in her own room, storing up reproaches and tears. Metiochos gave her no chance to use them. Silently he dropped down by her side and put his arm about her, burying his face in her lap. So unaccustomed was the gesture that Phaedime did not know what to make of it. She could only stroke the thick, dark hair, bending over him as though he were her child and not her master. Presently he said with a sighing groan, "Little Phaedime, what a man they have married you to! When they send for me, you had best go home to Susa."

Phaedime was alarmed, but she came from a long line of soldiers. "Wherever you go, I shall go too. I will even go to war if you will take me," Phaedime said.

Hippias's List

Datis, the King's general, was a thickset man whose lack of inches prevented him from looking down on Metiochos. Instead, he wrinkled his forehead in an insolent stare as he rumbled, "The horse transports are of my own devising. Greeks fight well on foot but have few horsemen. These Athenians will not expect us to bring our cavalry."

Metiochos smiled politely. His experience in battle had been small compared to that of Datis, who had fought in all the major campaigns of the great Greek rebellion. He remembered, however, that Miltiades used to declare Greek armies could have been victorious with better generalship. He contented himself with remarking to Datis that Attica was more rugged than Asia. Greek valleys, separated by narrow trails and precipitous passes, were neither wide nor numerous.

Datis made an impatient swat with his hand at a passing fly. His expression compared the young man to the buzzing insect. "Going by sea, we may choose our own ground for a landing. I understand my business very well. You may leave it to me."

This was openly rude. Datis's temper had been soured in recent years by his being demoted in favor of a young nephew of Darius. He was now restored to command; but Artaphernes, yet another of the King's nephews, had been joined with him. As the elder and more experienced, Datis deferred as little as he dared to Artaphernes. Nuisance, however, though the young man was, Datis did not consider him a rival for power in mainland Greece. Artaphernes was the son of the governor at Sardis and clearly destined to succeed to that position. To Datis, he appeared less dangerous than Metiochos, a husband of the King's niece and a Greek himself. Moreover, since Metiochos was unpopular with the King's connections, snubbing him was an easy way of pleasing Artaphernes.

All this was known to Metiochos, who affected not to notice Datis's rudeness. He took his leave and sought out Boubares, who had been appointed to command a thousand. To him he remarked in heated tones that Persians might pride themselves on being straightforward, but that in reality they liked intrigue as well as Greeks. The personality of the Great King kept them in order as long as they were under his eye. But now that the Great King grew old and ailing, mere messages could not control his commanders.

Boubares, who had established himself in an elaborate campaigning tent, pending the arrival of his thousand, twirled the points of his long moustaches and said nothing. He did not like to bring the name of Darius into a conversation which might seem critical of him. It offended his sense of honor.

Metiochos smiled ruefully. "Forgive me, friend. I lost my temper."

Boubares looked at him in surprise. "You've changed. I never knew you to give way to anger before."

Metiochos gave a short laugh. "On our journey to Susa together, there were fifty prisoners to whom I could say what I pleased — in Greek. Now there is no one."

Boubares took a sip of wine from the cup at his elbow. He seemed to consider. "They tell me that you scoured the slave markets for captives who were taken in your ship."

"The mines got most of them." Metiochos's tone was bitter. Slaves taken to the mines did not live long.

"An older man came my way." Boubares's tone was casual. "I bought him for your sake. One of the pursuing ships picked him out of the sea and — as sometimes happens — did not declare its booty with the rest. Being shorthanded, they put him on a rowing-bench and later, when they got back to Sidon, sold him off. He's yours if you want him. His name's Cleomenes."

"Cleo . . . Cleo . . . menes!" Metiochos started to laugh and had hard work to stop. To think of Boubares sheltering the architect of the great rebellion, a criminal on whose head a price was set! It was lucky that the Persian had been kept in Syria, where Datis was gathering the major part of his forces. Cleon's appearance would have been recognized in any city which looked on the Aegean.

"He'll have changed," Boubares said apologetically. "Great scar and walks with a limp. Most probably the Phoenicians knocked him about. Considering all, however, he's still spry."

Metiochos was at a loss for words. Boubares did not want thanks, but he had shown great understanding. Metiochos was fonder of Gergis, and indeed of Boubares himself, than of any friend he had made in Greece. In Bactria, Megabates had almost become his second father. Often he had wished that he were Persian, and yet he found that he was not. Now Boubares had perceived that only with Greeks could a Greek fully relax.

Metiochos smiled at his friend with eyes that were actually misted with unshed tears. He was aware that Cleon's presence in his household would put him in danger, but he had no thought of refusing the gift. He thirsted for the companionship of his own kind. He was intoxicated with secret joy that Cleon was not dead.

From this time on, Metiochos was aware that he and Cleon walked together on a cliff's edge which might

crumble beneath them. Cleon had put a knife scar
on his face which had twisted his lip. He had taught himself to walk with a limp and a hunch of the shoulder,
lest any recognize his height or gait. He had let his beard
grow longer, trimmed his eyebrows, altered the shape of
his hairline, and yellowed his skin. He kept his voice low
and affected an accent which he had picked up from a
Sicilian Greek. The Sidonians had many Sicilian slaves
because their colony of Carthage had waged a number of
wars against that island.

Metiochos took in the effect of these changes in a long,
thoughtful stare. When they were alone together, he
shook his head. "You're still Cleon."

Cleon used to spread his hands as he talked. The slave
Cleomenes held them close clasped together. But the
familiar eyes looked at him boldly from either side of the
long nose. "I was playing this game before you were born.
I was Cleophon then."

Metiochos paced uneasily across the room and back. In
the expedition against Athens, he was to command the
Greek contingent from the cities of the coast. It was un-
believable that a face known to so many would not be
recognized there. Cleon might keep his gaze on the
ground. There were drugs which women put into their
eyes to make them brighter and larger. Sooner or later,
however, he would betray himself. It would be wiser to
leave him behind with Phaedime who would reach Syria
as soon as the weather permitted easy travel. On the other
hand, the pleasure of being able to speak without thinking was an exquisite one. He hesitated.

"You'll spin intrigues behind my back, as you did to Miltiades."

Cleon's smile had turned into a sneer, curling up his malformed lip to show stained teeth. "I had my opportunity then. It has passed by. Not in my lifetime will the cities of the coast rebel again. As for the Athenians, why should I care about them if you do not?"

Metiochos went a dull red, but he was not yet ready to discuss the Athenians with Cleon. He made no promise that he would take the man with him, but pondered the matter. At Ephesos, whither he was bound to take up his command, Cleon's expert knowledge of personalities would surely be useful. Why trouble about one particular danger amid many?

Ephesos, where they arrived a few weeks later, had become the greatest city on the coast since the fall of Miletos. Here the expedition against Athens had created turmoil. Actual contingents had not yet arrived. The expense of maintaining armies had caused cities to delay their draft until the Persians set sail for Samos, where all were to assemble. Ships, however, were being prepared; and armorers were busy. Politicians of every sort were flocking to Ephesos in the hopes of winning favors from the commander.

Metiochos soon discovered anew that Greek intrigues were worse than Persian. For faction, the Greek cities of the coast were unmatched in the world. They were all democracies now. The great rebellion had forced the Persians to see that hated tyrants gave less stability than popular rule. Ever since the change, however, the governor at Sardis had been besieged by rival politicians. Since power depended chiefly on his favor, party struggle became more important than the general welfare.

Nothing could be done without endless argument. Metiochos, who had won the reputation of a silent man in Bactria, grew hoarse with discussion. Politics might be petty, but many of the leaders of the cities were more than mere politicians. One was a great poet, one a famous athlete. One was the son of a renowned philosopher. Many had traveled widely, both within and without the empire of the Persians. Such people did not need to labor small points. They won concessions because their company was an education. It was only surprising that they were content to be used in party squabbles.

Among the best of such leaders, Metiochos discovered that the coming conquest of mainland Greece was popular. A loose confederation had been forced on the coastal cities by the power of the governor at Sardis. Now that their tyrants were removed, all felt the good of a system which allowed each city independence, while preventing it harming the rest. Miltiades, too, had seen long ago that petty rivalries between Greek cities benefited no one. He had dreamed of establishing a north Aegean empire with the help of Oloros. His resources had not been sufficient for the task, but those of Darius might do Greece a greater service.

Such ideas were exciting. The peculiar greatness of the King, Metiochos argued, consisted neither in his position nor in his desire for further conquest. His ambition was as purely selfish as any other lust for power. But it was tempered by the knowledge that to rule so vast a dominion at all, he must rule well. He thought it necessary to understand foreign peoples and to protect their laws and customs. Was it not possible that Greeks could fulfill themselves inside such an empire?

Metiochos began to live again in the political atmosphere in which he had grown up. Even the necessity of punishing the Athenians was less distasteful because the leading men on the coast accepted it. Over Hippias they shook their heads, but took for granted that he would not live long. Meanwhile, they were thankful to see a son of Miltiades in command of their forces.

Greek politics were at the same time enlightened and petty. Underhand conspiracies flourished as well as lofty ideals. In Ephesos, Cleon kept himself in the background out of caution. He was seldom in company, while his supposed lameness gave him an excuse for never going out. Greeks, however, had an instinctive sense of political values. It was very soon rumored that the slave's opinion, though never voiced in public, had weight with his master. After experiment, another report went around that he was not bribable.

Among the foreigners settled in Ephesos was a certain Syracusan, who expressed a desire to meet his fellow Sicilian. He learned that Cleomenes had been born in Gela and had been a slave in Sidon for thirty years. Previous inquiries undertaken on his behalf had convinced him that he no longer had any relatives living. The story had the merit of being true in every respect, save that it belonged to Cleon. His identity had been adopted in Sidon, together with his accent.

Baffled, the merchant still persevered, professing nothing but homesickness and friendly feeling for a fellow exile. Cleon's goings and comings were unsupervised, it being the custom for Persian lords to treat their confidential servants as humble friends. Cleon was shortly pressed to dine with his new acquaintance, who promised to hire him a litter to spare his lameness.

"Be careful!" Metiochos warned when he heard of the invitation.

"I should like to know who is paying him," Cleon retorted. "It is unwise to reject a man you can see through, lest a more subtle one appear in his place."

The dinner party of the Syracusan proved excellent entertainment. The company was small and select. The wine was well chosen. Conversation ranged from the interpretation of dreams to the experiments of Pythagoras in dissecting animals. Never once did it become embarrassing by impinging on Metiochos's affairs. When the guests eventually departed, it was late. The Syracusan came out to see Cleon into his litter and took a cordial farewell. The link-boy started ahead, and the porters followed.

The central street of Ephesos, which ran through the marketplace, was recognizable for its famous public buildings. Side streets, however, were harder to distinguish. Narrow alleys were bounded by blank walls. Shop entrances were shuttered. Booths, built into the roadway as far as their owners dared, were closed up tight. Here and there the torch lit up a tiny square, a public fountain, or a little boundary stone with a rough image of a bearded god, one of hundreds throughout the city.

Through this confusing maze the link-boy threaded his way, the bearers following. He rapped with authority on a door, which was flung open. He stood aside. The bearers set the litter down for Cleon to alight.

Cleon got up slowly, at pains to move as befitted his lameness, even by the uncertain gleam of the boy's torch. Inside, the porter had let his lamp go out and was mumbling curses as he attempted to get a fresh spark. Cleon grasped the sides of the crude chair on which he had been sitting and began to lower himself onto the ground.

A hand came from behind to clap a cloth over his nose and mouth. A dagger pricked his ribs. "Do as you're told!" a voice rumbled. "You'll not come to harm. Don't try to cry out."

Cleon went limp and let two people lift him out of the litter and hustle him through the doorway, which was promptly slammed, cutting off the torchlight. In the darkness, he found himself cramped into a small vestibule with people stinking of garlic crowded against him.

"Blind him!" ordered a voice, no longer troubling to lower its tone. The cloth was removed from his mouth and, while he gasped for breath, bound quickly around his eyes and knotted behind. Hands held his elbows so that he could not interfere.

"This way!" They pushed him across a sandy court and what might have been the pavement of a colonnade.

Through the stuffy darkness of the cloth over eyes and nose, he comprehended that he had reached a lamplit room. They pushed a stool against his legs, and he sat gratefully. He had not found it easy to move as though he were lame when half off balance. His elbows were still held, but he put his hands down and fingered the stool. Its seat was of fine leather and there was inlay work on the curved wood. It told him nothing except that those who had laid this trap were wealthy.

Papyrus rustled. Somebody before him was folding up a scroll. While he did so, nothing happened.

A cold, dry, elderly voice broke the silence. "This then is the slave . . . Sicilian, eh?"

The sudden sharpness of the tone demanded an answer. Cleon nodded.

"Hm, yes. Sicilian . . . slave in Sidon thirty years?" There was a cool quality about this voice which Cleon did not like, but he nodded again. His was a circumstantial story and hard to be shaken.

"How long with your present lord?"

Cleon's heart leaped with sudden fright. He was tempted to claim three years, but Metiochos's household had almost certainly been questioned. He compromised. "My master bought me before he went to Bactria because I was Greek. But discovering I was not fit to ride so far, he lent me to his friend until he returned. Lately he brought me by ship from the Cilician coast."

"You have served him, then, a month or two; but you are not bribable. Why?"

It was a good question. Cleon shrugged in answer.

"It is not conceivable that you are devoted."

Cleon ran his tongue across his lips. "Not devoted, no. Frightened."

"Ah!" It was a sigh of understanding. This old man knew how to deal with frightened people.

"Look at me!" Cleon burst into frantic speech. "Look at my leg, my face, my shoulder. Strip me and examine the marks! Can't you see I've been put to the torture!"

"Ah!" That little sigh again. "Once frightened, always frightened, eh? I have seen it happen."

"I'll not risk pain again! You don't know what it is!"

"But I do," the elderly voice retorted gently. "I know very well."

Cleon swallowed. He tried to shrink together into his clothes, but he said nothing.

"You are afraid of the wrong man," his tormentor said. "You know your master, but you do not know who we are. You cannot avoid us. I have poisons which eat out men's insides, a little every day. I have cellars into which people suddenly vanish and never reappear. I have men in my pay in your master's very household. Strange accidents will happen to you. Unless you help us, I give you my word that you will suffer pain."

Cleon shook his head, mouth hanging open. "I don't dare!"

Papyrus rustled again as though elderly fingers were smoothing it out flat. "You will dare. When you are ready to do what we wish, tell the Syracusan. I warn you, he knows nothing, save how to pass a message on." He opened the papyrus more decisively and said to those who held Cleon, "Take the slave home."

Metiochos received an account of this adventure the following evening after a long day. He looked incredulously at Cleon, who merely hunched up one shoulder in a gesture belonging to his disguise. To demand services with threats and then do nothing seemed less than rational. Metiochos wondered if someone was playing a practical joke.

"Whatever did they want?" he asked, astonished.

Cleon drew up his shoulder higher than ever, pressing his arm to his side and bowing over it as though it hurt him. "I suppose he wanted to know if you have messengers from Athens. Perhaps, too, some of the exiles may prefer you to a mad tyrant and his foolish grandson. Hippias grows jealous."

"Hippias!" Metiochos was blankly astonished. "He's in Samos, which is more convenient for messages coming from Athens. What possible connection lies between your adventure in Ephesos and that old tyrant?"

Cleon sighed. "Samos is not far off. Wherever Hippias may be this morning, it is certain he was in Ephesos last night. I spoke with him."

"How can you be sure? One old man sounds like another. They whistle because they have lost front teeth, and their voices quaver."

"I did not recognize him." Cleon had twisted up his lip in his strange, sneering smile. "Among the guests of my Sicilian merchant was a young man who did not claim to be Sicilian. Pale eyes, pale skin, pale hair he had. I first saw Hippias when he was just that age. As soon as the bearers set me down at the wrong door, I started to wonder if Hippias desired to see me himself. When I was sure, I knew I could deceive him if I could make him believe that I was frightened. It is Hippias's weakness to think that all men can be governed by fear."

"And you convinced him?"

"I believe so. Did he not promise me that I should suffer pain?" Cleon put back his cloak to reveal the arm he had been nursing. It was raw, red, and blistered from elbow to wrist.

Metiochos started in dismay. "He put that on you?" He was all the more angry because he had felt impatient with Cleon's affectations when the two of them were alone together.

"Let us call it an accident. This morning outside my room a lamp left burning fell over and poured hot oil across my arm. I made an outcry loud enough to suggest my nerve was being broken." He shook his head with a gesture of unconcern. "Do not look black because a servant in your household has taken Hippias's pay to torment me. New favorites such as I are always unpopular. Someone is jealous. Presently I shall give in and send a mesage to the Syracusan."

Metiochos consented to let the matter take its course. He was frantically busy and knew that Cleon was more than a match for people who considered him to be an elderly slave and frightened of pain. Moreover, if Hippias was planning trouble, he needed to know it. It was both his duty and his interest to restrain the aged tyrant.

In the next few days he had no time to question Cleon. The contingents were assembling at last. He was determined to be at Samos in advance of the main fleet and with his men in good order. His whole position depended on the efficiency of his command, since Datis would report his slightest failure and curtail his authority if given an excuse.

Nothing more was said between the two men on the subject of Hippias until the very eve of their sailing when Metiochos, returning home in the early hours of the morning, found Cleon sitting up. He blinked at him. Dizzy with fatigue and aching in every limb, he had no ambition for anything but sleep.

"Won't it wait till tomorrow?"

"Till Samos?" Cleon opened his hands in one of the small gestures which were all that Cleomenes permitted himself. "I don't know. What's this list?"

"List?" Metiochos was tired enough to be stupid. "Which one?" He had lists of contingents, of stores, of ships, of horses — endless lists.

"The list of names which Hippias has. Your cousin Lysias is on it." Lysias was one of the relatives of Hippias who had followed him into exile. He had passed through Ephesos on his way to join the band of Athenian exiles collecting around their old tyrant. He had taken advantage of his opportunity to call on Metiochos, to whom he was closer kin than to Hippias himself. His appearance had been duly reported by Cleon to the Syracusan, who had, it now appeared, shrugged careless shoulders and replied, "Don't trouble yourself about Lysias. He doesn't count any more. He's on the list."

Metiochos suggested crossly it was not unreasonable for Hippias to keep a list of his supporters. He himself would have to get up in three hours and was going to bed. It did dimly cross his mind that Lysias, expressing cautiously a fear that Hippias was growing old, had mentioned a list. Perhaps the old man's memory was slipping. Lysias had sounded dubious of his fitness to rule.

The setting out of the expedition and its arrival that afternoon at Samos drove such thoughts from his head. The larger fleet under Datis and Artaphernes was expected momentarily, and great efforts were needed to tidy the harbor for its reception. When it appeared, the work of organization had to be redone. Metiochos threw himself into his task, knowing that Datis watched.

There was little need to wonder what Hippias was doing in Samos. He was much in evidence, always surrounded by a gang of friends and fellow exiles. In appearance, he was if possible older than ever. He had shrunk together, and yellowish scalp showed through his thinning hair. But he still sat a horse and liked to carry a spear, though he could no longer bear the weight of armor. He was often in conference with Datis, boasting of his messages from Athens, where the people, so he said, were longing to receive their former lord.

Toward Metiochos he employed the flattering manner he was apt to use with those he most suspected. Leaning on his arm, he praised the order of the Greek contingents. He recalled with affection his cousin, dear Leucippe, who would have been proud of her son, had she lived to see this day. He invited his cousin, his colleague, his friend to take wine in his tent.

It suited Metiochos to agree because Datis inclined to follow Hippias's advice and land at Marathon. There was nothing against this except Metiochos's personal uneasiness and his suspicion that Hippias exaggerated his following in Athens. The arguments which had convinced Datis were plausible. Miltiades would march out of Athens and do battle on the open plain, where Datis's cavalry and archers would have the advantage. He must do this because he dared not trust the populace in a defensive war, seeing that the democracy was riddled with faction. As soon as he left, Hippias's partisans would rise inside the city. Miltiades would be caught between the two and cut to pieces.

Irritated at the constant mention of his father's name which put him in an embarrassing position, Metiochos had incautiously protested that Miltiades was not the Athenian general. Hippias had scornfully replied that by a provision of this ridiculous democracy there were ten generals, of whom Miltiades was certainly one. The War Leader, who presided over this unwieldy board, would be guided by Miltiades's advice. He knew the man.

Fuming, Metiochos perceived he was outmaneuvered. By protesting about a minor point on which he could be put in the wrong, he had lost authority to criticize the general plan. Datis was not disposed to listen to him now, and Artaphernes sought every occasion to show how he resented recognizing the Greek as a cousin by marriage.

Baffled, but by no means despairing, Metiochos sought out Hippias. His arrival was greeted with the same kind of effusion as he had encountered in public. But even resting, as he now was, in the shade of an awning outside his campaigning tent, Hippias was not alone. Besides his grandson, he had two nephews with him, sons of a half-brother whom Metiochos had particularly disliked. His son-in-law, once tyrant of Lampsacos, had also sent two children who might be considered rival claimants to Pisistratos for the succession. In addition, there were three men who had been the tyrant's agents, commanders of his bowmen, of his army of spies, of his secret assassins, and of all the apparatus of tyranny. Honest Athenians choked when they spoke of these, and Hippias had been advised to leave them behind. Here they were, lounging beside him on the grass, while Lysias and other aristocrats of decent background were conspicuous by absence.

Metiochos had been warned by Cleon what to expect and was not surprised, but he was disgusted. Cleon had wound himself into the confidence of Hippias's agents in a manner surprising only to those who did not know the man. He had shaken his head when Metiochos announced his intention of trying to reason with the old tyrant.

"He is beyond reason," Cleon said, "and he does not love you. But when he will not listen, you may ask him to show you the list which he conceals in his tent."

"The list again! What list?"

Cleon was elusive. "Better let it surprise you. Ask to see it."

Metiochos thought of this as he drank with Hippias, but

a chance did not seem to arise. The old man looked tired and confused. The chatter of his hangers-on monopolized the conversation while he sat brooding, head down and mouth slightly open, as though he had gone to sleep without shutting his eyes. Metiochos, who had never seen him otherwise than active, was disconcerted. However, he made a remark about the Marathon landing. It was not answered. Persevering, he tried again, pitching his voice a little louder.

"Eh, what?" The old man blinked and seemed to come to his senses. "Marathon? A good plan, eh?" He leaned forward and put a hand on Metiochos's knee. "D'you know, cousin, I had a dream last night. I dreamed I was going to sleep in my mother's bed. Now what can that be but a promise from the gods that I'll lay my bones forever in the land where I was born? I'll win back Athens yet!" His voice rose and trembled with the intensity of his desire, and one of the yellow teeth left in his upper jaw actually quivered as he spoke. Fascinated, Metiochos thought he was going to spit it out, but he did not. "What do you think of that, cousin, eh, for a good omen?"

Metiochos pursed his lips. One might die and be buried in defeat as well as in victory, but he did not want to upset the old man's confidence. "When the gods send dreams or visions," he said, "it is wise to pay attention. Now I also have had a vision, twice waking and sometimes in dreams, about Marathon. The first time . . ."

Hippias was not listening. He was staring into space with a dull, abstracted look as though he were for the moment in suspended animation. Metiochos told his tale, and he told it well. But the only interest it received was from one of the Lampsacos grandsons, who remarked that everybody knew a battle could not be fought without killing someone. For his part, if the gods were kind enough to tell him beforehand that he was going to die, he should stay at home, if only to discover what the gods would do then. The remark was greeted by a roar of flippant laughter which aroused Hippias again. He leaned forward and put a hand on Metiochos's knee. "D'you know, cousin, I had a dream last night . . ." The information was conveyed in exactly the same words as before, with the same conclusion, "What do you think of that, cousin, eh, for a good omen?"

Metiochos gave a sickly smile. His discomforture, as he could see, delighted the audience. Hippias's family was less concerned to bolster his dignity than to score off the people they disliked. No one who had seen Hippias in such a mood could imagine that he was fit to rule, but they did not care. The decisions would not be his when they had once gained power. Metiochos, looking around on them, felt a surge of loathing. They were like vultures circling above a dying Athens.

Remembering Cleon's advice, he gripped Hippias roughly by the arm and shook him a little. "Cousin, I have business with you today. Show me your list!"

There was a dead silence for a few seconds. Hippias blinked. The significance of the request seemed to dawn on him slowly. He withdrew his arm from Metiochos's grasp and smiled evilly. "Nobody sees my list until it is finished."

"Not even the executioners," agreed Pisistratos.

Hippias chuckled at this remark and nodded approval. "There's many a man on my list who has no suspicion that he is marked for death. I'll kill them all!"

Metiochos sprang up as if he had been pushed off his seat. It stood to reason that Hippias had enemies whom he wished to kill, but this cold-blooded scratching down of names revolted him. Hippias in senility was bad enough, but Hippias in madness was a poisonous spider, fit only to be stepped on.

"More than five thousand names," said Hippias, looking slyly about him at his friends, as though to tease them with the thought that one and all might be on it.

Charmides, who was the worst of a bad lot, shrugged his shoulders in open indifference, clearly conscious that whatever names Hippias might write, he would be needed to direct the murders and grow fat on confiscations. The gesture was not lost on the old man. "You think I am playing with you! You'll see! I'll read you some names." He got up and tottered into his tent.

Metiochos looked around on the group as the old man vanished. "Is Hippias often like this?"

"Sometimes," retorted Charmides with indifferent insolence. "It does not matter."

Hippias came out of his tent with a roll of papyrus long enough to have been a book clutched to his chest. His quivering fingers were starting to undo it when Metiochos put a hand over his shoulder and plucked it away.

"Nobody reads my list until it is finished," screamed Hippias, clutching after it. Metiochos merely held him off with one hand, while with the other he tried to spread out part of the roll in order to read it.

"Kill him and take it away!"

Metiochos lost patience. With a thrust of the arm he sent Hippias flying against Charmides, who was getting up. "Sit down, you dogs! Or do you want to reckon with the vengeance of the Great King? I have orders to oversee what will be done in Athens, and I shall read this list."

He unfolded it and glanced down it with horror. Every Athenian of any note seemed listed on it, including men Hippias could never have known. "Euphorion of the district of Eleusis," he read in a slow wonder. "This Euphorion is a blameless man who once befriended me. I remember him well. His sons, Cynegairos and Aeschylos, the poet. These were children when Hippias went into exile. What harm have they done him?"

He looked at Hippias, who had recovered his balance and even apparently some of his wits after the shaking. At all events, he returned Metiochos's look with more intelligence than he had shown that day. "Give me my staff," he muttered.

He took the staff and walked a few steps forward beyond the circle of trodden grass in front of his tent. It was already summer, so that the flowers which sprang up everywhere in spring were dying off. There were, however, tall thistles flowering still, and withered spikes of asphodel rose above the drying turf. Hippias swept his staff from side to side and beat himself a path.

"Cut down the tallest, cousin." He turned about to face Metiochos. "Do not spare the thistle because it has not pricked you yet. Cut down the tallest."

"I see." Metiochos's voice was dry. "Let us then examine the district of Marathon. Ah, yes . . . Aristias, son of Arion, Olympic winner . . . Poor old fool . . . Conon, son of Callicrates . . . You killed his father and so, of course, must kill the son. There's logic in it . . . Miltiades, son of Cimon, and Cimon his son . . ." He crumpled the roll angrily. "How dare you, when Miltiades's life is given to me?"

Hippias scowled at him, silent but not repentant. In imagination, Metiochos could see him in his tent that evening wetting his reed pen to add to the names of the district, "Metiochos, son of Miltiades." His intention was plain as though it had been expressed.

With slow deliberation, Metiochos began to tear up the roll. He tore it crosswise, then lengthwise, then into ever smaller pieces which fell on the ground like a shower of petals between himself and Hippias. Names and fragments of names stared up at him . . . Lysias his cousin, who had gone into exile for Hippias's sake and whose fault probably lay in protesting against a savage vengeance . . . Chrysippos, who was his own mother's brother's son and married to a niece of Hippias . . . It seemed possible that the old tyrant really had forgotten that he must leave some men alive over whom to rule.

Metiochos flung down the last shreds and dusted his hands, as though after contact with a foul thing. "There'll be no killing without my permission," he said and turned away. Behind him, Charmides shrugged his shoulders.

"We know what we have to do. Who cares for a list?"

The Landing

Near the southern tip of Euboea, where that long narrow island stretches down the Attic coast from the northwest, Datis called a council of war to acquaint his commanders with the shape of the Marathon plain and his choice of a landing. It was a fair day near the end of July. From the slight elevation where Datis had pitched his tent, the captains of his thousands could look down on a narrow coastal plain, thickly dotted with the campfires of their army and bordered on the seaward side by a long fringe of ships. Slightly inland, the horses were cropping the brown turf, through which a little river, hardly ankle-deep at this time of year, meandered seaward. Northward behind hills a wisp of smoke rose slowly from the ruins of Eretria. After sacking that city, Datis had drawn his army off to spare his soldiers the stench of unburied enemies. He had taken captive all survivors and herded them onto uninhabited islets between Euboea and the mainland, where they could be guarded until his transports started homeward. All this had been completed three days ago, but Eretria still smoked. Metiochos with an inward sigh sat down in a position where he could not see it.

The fleet had sailed from Samos in good spirits, and it had come to the islands which were called the Cyclades. Famous among these was Delos, venerated as the birthplace of the sun god Apollo. Datis conquered the rest of the Cyclades with little trouble, and he plundered where resistance had been made. On Delos, however, he would not permit his soldiers to land. Instead, he sent over costly frankincense to be burned on Apollo's altar.

Such reverence for the sacred place delighted the Greek contingents. In addition, they had long desired to have the Cyclades, who were commercial rivals, brought under control. Enthusiasm soared as they sailed for Euboea.

There were no great cities in Euboea, but a number of small ones. Some put up a token resistance. Others deserted homes and farms to flee to the mainland. A few submitted, and to these Datis was gracious. The Eretrians alone held out in desperation. These Eretrians were old allies of the Athenians and had helped them with five

ships on their fatal expedition against Sardis. Now therefore they knew they could expect no mercy, and they
vowed to die where they were born.

Around Eretria the Persian army surged like an angry
sea. Mounds of earth were piled against the walls. Rams
battered them. Tunnels undermined them. Scaling ladders were planted against them and thrown down. The
besieged, countering night assault with pre-dawn sorties,
took no rest. Their women labored side by side with the
men, repairing their walls.

Such an unequal conflict could have but one ending.
Meanwhile, however, casualties among the besiegers rose
high. The Greeks under Metiochos's command lost heart.
In part they were affected by the grumbles of unwilling
reinforcements from the Cyclades, whom Datis had
drafted as hostages for the islands' good behavior. Besides, the leaders of the coastal democracies had used
the expedition as a chance to see the back of political rivals. It naturally followed that the further these got
from home, the more anxious they became about what
went on there. In particular, they feared to earn unpopu-
larity by destroying Eretria, whose democracy was on
friendly terms with the coastal cities.

The efforts of the Greek contingents visibly slackened,
and Metiochos found his position growing awkward. At
the council meeting he made up his mind to say nothing.
The Marathon landing was the plan of Hippias, to
whom he had never spoken since their quarrel in Samos.

This council meeting was one of Hippias's good days.
Nobody who heard him discussing a rising in Athens

could imagine the incoherence which overcame him in
the privacy of his tent. To be sure, his grandson and Charmides sat beside him, ready to remove him if he lost the
thread of his discourse. On subjects of his own choosing,
however, Hippias could hold his own, provided he were
not cut short or confused by a question which did not fit
into his discourse. Datis, who sincerely admired the old
man's abilities, said outright that he wished all Greeks
showed equal loyalty. He gave no side glance as he spoke,
but the remark created a silence. Metiochos was popular
with the commanders of thousands, friends of Boubares,
and also with the leaders of the Greeks.

Charmides had taken Hippias by the elbow and was
whispering to him. Everyone could see that he was urging something and that Hippias, nodding his beard at
the end of every sentence, was agreeing. The old man got
to his feet again and started a rambling denunciation of
his cousin, son of Miltiades, and lukewarm against the
King's enemies. He did not mention the list Metiochos
had torn up because, with the instinct of long practice,
he liked to conceal his own cold-bloodedness. In general
terms, however, he dwelt on the vengeance which he must
take on his own foes and those of the Great King.

Metiochos let Hippias sputter on, losing coherence as
he gained vehemence. Presently, when the venom of the
old man had been sufficiently displayed, he interrupted
without rising from his place. "To kill is easy. Hippias
should rather consider over whom he wants to rule, lest
when he has made an example of all his enemies, he have
no subjects left."

There was laughter among the captains at this sally. Red mounted into Hippias's yellow cheeks; and he stuttered, dribbling out of the corner of his mouth into his beard. Charmides, who perceived that his master was beside himself with fury and could not come to the point, spoke out of turn, he having no command of a contingent or a thousand. "Is the Great King's revenge to be turned into a joke? Such words come fittingly from Metiochos, seeing that he has already stolen an Eretrian from among the King's captives and smuggled him to the mainland."

Metiochos went red in his turn, for he had imagined this kindness had been performed in secrecy. Calmly he put a good face on the matter. "The King gave me freely the lives of my own kin. This Tisander I rescued is my cousin whom I have known since a child."

Datis scowled, but Metiochos met his gaze with no sign of concern. Inwardly he knew that the commander was asking himself whether he dared lay hands on the King's nephew. Darius was jealous of his rights and would brook no interference between himself and prisoners. On the other hand, Datis knew only in general terms what had been granted to Metiochos and what to Hippias. Boldly the young man added, "My cousin Tisander was too old and ill to survive a journey to Susa. Therefore, since the King gave me his life . . ." He shrugged careless shoulders.

"Tisander was no Athenian," cried Charmides in anger. "Nothing was said by the King about Eretrian cousins. If it had been, why should the matter have been kept a secret?"

Metiochos got up and went over to Charmides in an unhurried way which gave no hint of his intention. He did not draw the sword which hung at his belt, well knowing that he would put himself in the wrong if he did so in the council. Instead, before anyone could stop him, he drew up his fist and crashed it into Charmides's face, lifting the man clear off his feet and turning his mouth into a ruin of bloodied lips and broken teeth. Charmides fell on his back in the dust, while Metiochos, whose own knuckles were cut to the bone, turned angrily on Datis.

"By what right does this dog speak in council? Is he to pursue a private quarrel while we make plans for a war? Must our deliberations be muddied by such filth?"

Datis bit his lip. No captain had stirred from his place to help Charmides, who sat spitting out blood and dabbling his lips with the hem of his tunic, unwilling to rise to his feet while Metiochos stood over him. The staff of Hippias trembled in his hand with impotent rage. He thumped it on the ground, appealing to Datis. "This man is my servant."

"Then he should hold his tongue before his betters," replied Datis in cold tones. His dignity had been impaired because he had permitted Charmides to speak without rebuke. He saw that the sense of the meeting was against him.

Far quicker in decision than the general, Metiochos seized his advantage. "If there is nothing further that needs to be said about the landing, you will permit me to take my leave." He turned on his heel and walked away, leaving an uproar behind him as the captains joined in berating Charmides. Nevertheless, before the army embarked on the following morning, Metiochos received three warnings.

The first of these was from Boubares, gently given yet with the authority of the captains behind it. Let Metiochos remember that the general was the Great King's deputy. Metiochos did not mistake the purport of this, which was to tell him that the captains, though they liked him, would not support him against Datis. On the heels of this came a message from Datis himself, cried so loudly that it was spread through the camp. Miltiades and what other kin Metiochos might claim must travel to Susa to be judged by the Great King. They were not to go free. The third warning was the most disquieting of all. It came from Cleon. Pisistratos, into whose council he had wormed himself, had asked Cleon if he had any cousins among the Greeks of the coast. "You remind Charmides of someone he once knew," Pisistratos had said.

Metiochos, who had gradually come to feel safe about Cleon, suffered a shock. "Why Charmides?"

Cleon was indifferent. "Does that matter? I said my mother was a woman of Priene, but since my father had quarreled with hers over a matter of business, I did not know what kin she had."

"And did that satisfy Pisistratos?"

Cleon looked at him slyly out of those too familiar eyes. "At all events, it will not satisfy Charmides. He will make inquiries, and other people will be found to have had suspicions. Presently he will be certain, but he will not act until he has proof."

Metiochos agreed. In the confusion of the landing and
the campaign against Athens, Charmides might not have
the leisure time. All the same, if the case of Tisander had
not warned Metiochos how carefully he was watched, he
would have urged Cleon to make his escape for the sake
of them both.

Spirits soon rose with the need for action. To Metiochos's relief, the landing was not made on the south
beach, where a boy had heard shadows whisper of disaster. Hippias preferred the north beach for excellent reasons. It had better anchorage for ships, which were protected by a natural breakwater at this end of the bay.
The northern campsite was sheltered behind a great
marsh and had good grazing for horses. Datis could not
be attacked where he was, but might sally when he
pleased.

The Athenian exiles had hired themselves a special
ship which they had garlanded with boughs of olive and
myrtle for the landing. Fluteplayers were giving their
oarsmen the time. In the waist of the ship, a half-dozen
snow-white lambs were waiting to be sacrificed on the
beach, especially to Athene and Poseidon and to Hercules,
who had a sacred precinct in a grove of trees at the south
end of the plain. Conspicuous on the prow stood Hippias,
the wind fluttering his beard and wispy hair as he reminded his comrades how a dream had promised that his
bones should rest forever in the land where he was born.

The Athenian ship ran up the beach, and its rowers
jumped out smartly. A plank was put out for Hippias to
descend onto his native soil. The flute-players struck up

a fresh tune as the old tyrant moved along the gangway and mounted the side of the ship, looking down on the sand.

The plank was steep and the old man's legs were feeble. Only by dropping his staff and clutching at his grandson did he avoid descending at a run to topple head foremost. As it was, the narrow escape brought on a fit of coughing which prevented him from saying anything as his foot touched Attic shore. His people hustled him inland, while he resisted, choking for breath. Thus his first intelligible words were not the prayer of thanksgiving which he had composed for the occasion. They were simply a quivering cry of alarm: "My tooth! My tooth!"

Attendants tried to soothe the old man, but he would not be quiet. His loose tooth had fallen out; and he was beside himself with senile alarm, lest the promise which he had received in a dream be already fulfilled. A tooth of him was buried forever in Attic land. He set men to quartering the sand on hands and knees and could hardly be brought to attend to the sacrifices. The occasion, which was to have been a solemn one, was turned into farce. All the fleet was giggling at him, indifferent to the bad omen. Hippias it appeared was popular with no one. His quarrel with Metiochos especially had alienated all the Greek contingents.

Mount Pentelicos, which dominated the southern end of the plain, was visible from Athens over twenty miles away. On Pentelicos, as the ships had turned in toward the bay, the smoke of signal fires had been going up. By the following morning as soon as it was light, the cavalry scouts whom Datis had sent forward to keep watch on the plain reported movement along the coast road coming up from Athens. The tribal detachments were pouring along it at full speed and must have been marching for most of the night. Since their rations and the heavy parts of their armor were being carried by porters, who encumbered their ranks, the cavalry squadrons had them at a disadvantage. In a series of brushes, the Athenians lost a number of men. They pressed on, however, protected by the olive groves and clumps of brushwood which bordered the southern slopes of Pentelicos.

As the sun rose high, Datis withdrew his cavalry, whose full strength he did not wish to betray. His hopes, however, that the Athenians would draw up in line of battle were disappointed. They turned inland to the grove of Hercules at the foot of wooded hills, whence they commanded the road by which they had come and a rugged hill path leading round the back of Pentelicos to Athens. Having thus secured their communications, they began felling trees which they arranged trunks inward and branches towards the enemy, presenting a tangle impenetrable to cavalry raids. Then safely encamped, they left to Datis choice of action.

The captains of the thousands and especially the commanders of the cavalry were disappointed. Artaphernes, who was the leader of these, pressed for action. Datis, however, preferred a waiting game. "Now let the Athenians rise for Hippias, and their army will be at our mercy," said he.

Metiochos fell upon this statement, remarking drily

that Hippias had overestimated his popularity in Athens. The old tyrant, whose powers had visibly declined since the day of the landing when he had lost his tooth, was hardly able to defend his promises. Pisistratos, speaking for him, pointed out that the hillfolk, among whom the tyrant's supporters lay, took time to gather. In addition they were cut off from Marathon plain by the position of the Athenians astride the hill path. Messages had undoubtedly been sent. They would come in by a roundabout route.

Metiochos looked around on the inner council, which consisted of half a dozen men, of whom he was the only Greek in high command. Among these people he knew that no one wished him well, but he had a duty to his own captains. Defiantly he threw up his head. "We wait for Hippias, and he waits for his friends. Meanwhile, the Athenians are waiting likewise. Have you asked yourselves what they are waiting for inside their hedge?"

Artaphernes laughed scornfully. "They are terrified of our cavalry, which they never expected to see. They dare not attack us."

Metiochos shook his head almost pityingly. "Oh no! Everybody who tumbled into a boat and fled from Euboea knew perfectly well that we had horsemen with us. The Athenians had counted our ships and numbered our divisions long before their beacons burned on Pentelicos. If, knowing what they did, they marched against us, I say again, why do they wait once they are here?"

"I maintain they dare not face us. Give me the cavalry, and I'll throw fire on their hedge and smoke them out."

Artaphernes by the splendor of his appearance looked like a king's nephew. His haughty manner gave his opinions weight. Datis, whose instructions had been to share command with this prince, nodded slowly. But before committing himelf, he looked at Metiochos, raising his eyebrows in a question.

Metiochos had long ago lost awe of Datis, whom he thought slow to make decisions and too accustomed to easy triumphs like that over the Cyclades. On the whole, he preferred the judgment of Artaphernes, though he did not imagine the cavalry would accomplish much unless the army were moved across the plain in support. Both commanders despised their enemy too easily, forgetting that Athens was several times the size of Eretria and that the hatred of the Athenians for Hippias gave edge to their resolution.

"The Athenians are waiting," he pointed out, "for the coming of the Spartans, to whom they will have sent runners as soon as Eretria fell. The Spartans are not used to hanging back from war, and they are fighters such as those who despise Greek armies have never encountered. With their arrival, our forces may be equaled or outnumbered."

Datis looked concerned, as well he might. Hippias, however, with a flash of the intelligence he still could show, dismissed the Spartans with an impatient wave of the hand. "Never mind them yet! I know them well. The Spartans are keeping the sacred festival of Apollo. They will never march in the holy month before the full of the moon."

Pisistratos chimed in to agree. Even Metiochos was

forced to admit that since the Spartans had not already appeared, it was most probable that they had delayed their setting out. Considering, however, that the full moon was now at hand, they might be expected within seven days. Meanwhile, as Hippias vowed, the rising in Athens on which he fixed his hopes would surely take place.

Datis consented to wait, though the risk he was taking sent Metiochos back to his quarters in a thoughtful mood. To his captains he showed a cheerful face, but to Cleon he confided that delay was likely to put them all in danger.

Cleon rubbed his hands. "Good, good!" he exclaimed. "Give the word when you are ready, and we'll go over to Miltiades."

"Go . . . over!" Metiochos's jaw dropped open. He had considered the chance that Cleon might desert him now, but this suggestion bereft him of words. The Greek contingents, who depended utterly on him, would be cut to pieces if mismanaged by their ignorant commanders.

"Nonsense!" he snapped.

Cleon looked at him sideways, but he did not pursue the matter. He said quietly, "A week's delay will give Charmides time to make inquiries. He will find people prepared to swear they know me well. What then?"

To this there was no answer. Metiochos made none. But he knew, and Cleon knew, that a crisis was coming.

Without the Cavalry

FOR SOME DAYS Persian cavalry scouts roamed the plain, venturing to the edge of the brushwood thicket, emboldened by the absence of Athenian cavalry. A few daring spirits approached close enough to discharge arrows at random against the camp inside. The scattering of ill-aimed missiles which answered them showed that the Athenians had not even brought along the Scythian bowmen who had once been mercenaries of Hippias. This information was received with joy by their old tyrant. The bowmen, he pointed out to Datis, had not been trusted — and with reason. They were deep in the plot to stage a coup in Athens.

Datis grunted without pleasure. He knew the captains of his thousands were gnawing their nails with frustration. Their army was superior in weapons and tactics. It also outnumbered the Athenians, as had been obvious when the latter had defiled onto the plain. The Persian cavalry remembered the King's cupbearer at the great feasts crying to his master, "Sire, remember the Athenians!" They saw this battle as an affair of honor, and thus longed to begin it. Only that morning Datis had seen a word scratched in the dust outside his tent which his men had not rubbed out. It had been, "Sardis."

Hippias perceived the general's annoyance but was too good a politician to take notice. To him, the great thing was, Datis had not moved yet. Hippias, who trusted no one, feared lest Datis push him aside when victory was won. The tyrant's position would be greatly strengthened if his partisans took Athens. For this reason he was profuse with reassurances. His friends would soon be ready to strike. A battle could then follow.

"Last night was the full moon," pointed out Datis, still surly. "The Spartans will be setting out this morning." He was angry because it had cost him something to hold out for inaction in face of the pressure put on him by Artaphernes. So far, moreover, he had nothing to show for his trust in the promises of Hippias. The only messages which the tyrant had received from his friends in Athens were frantic appeals for delay. The conspirators were either more timorous or far less powerful than Hippias pretended.

Hippias was eager to seem confident. His friends also had their eye on the moon. They knew that victory must be won before the Spartans could arrive. Let Datis have patience for another twenty-four hours!

Scowling reluctantly, Datis nodded. He had already decided he could afford to wait another day, provided that nothing thereafter went wrong. The uprising, if it really would take place, was vital to him. Any siege must be interrupted by the Spartans. Besides, if Datis were to move now, he would be thought to have yielded to Artaphernes, who would claim credit for the victory.

Datis glowered, therefore, but he waited a long morning while the soldiers played interminable gambling games, the captains grumbled, and the narrow campsite grew dirtier with use. In no section was discontent greater than among the Greek units, though these were not staring with eagerness across the plain, but with longing at the sea which divided them from home. To the fury of Metiochos, the story of Hippias's list was being told everywhere, with the addition that, since it had been torn up, Hippias had made another which was headed by Metiochos's name. Such enthusiasm as the Greeks had originally felt for the conquest of Athens was completely destroyed by this gossip, which Metiochos indignantly accused Cleon of spreading.

Without the slightest change of expression, Cleon denied it, pointing out that the retainers of the tyrant were fools enough to have betrayed it themselves. Metiochos was forced to admit this was possible, but he was not satisfied. He himself had imbibed something of the Persian attitude towards lying, as being in itself evil. More pragmatic, Cleon lied without scruple when occasion demanded. Metiochos had lost confidence in Cleon since the moment when he had suggested that they change sides, implying that the action was one he had intended from the beginning.

Cleon seemed to read his thoughs. "The Greek contingents will not fight willingly for Hippias. Why, then, do you?"

Metiochos glowered. It occurred to him that once he had wept because Cleon was living. Now he cursed the occasion when they had met again and would have put the man under guard were he not fearful of attracting any attention to his servant. "Get me something to eat," he ordered curtly, snatching at an excuse to get rid of his presence.

Cleon turned to leave the tent, but he paused with his hand on the curtain and said softly, "All your life I have watched over you. I sent you to your father when Tisander would have returned you to Athens. I protected you when Oloros showed he was jealous. I taught you what politics are and how to lead men. We met for the first time when you were six years old, and you had a bold spirit then. I wished I had a son like you, but I never imagined that you would be a willing slave to the Great King."

Metiochos neither moved nor spoke, and Cleon went

out. Without waiting to eat the food he had ordered, Metiochos left the tent to look for Boubares.

The Persian was not in his own tent, but with the captains of his hundreds who, like the rank and file, camped
in the open. Metiochos sat down, shaking his head at
their looks of inquiry. "No meeting of the inner council,
and no news."

"Hippias was with the commander just now," Boubares
remarked.

One of the captains spat. Whether on account of the
delay or for other reasons, Hippias it seemed was not popular here either.

"Last night was the full of the moon," Boubares urged.
Impatience for action was riding him like all the rest.
There was nothing more to be said about the Spartans, yet
Boubares could not keep off the subject. In the idleness
of these days of waiting, there had been too much talk.
The very camp followers had their ideas on strategy.

Metiochos said nothing because there was nothing to
say. The captains of the hundreds, out of deference to
his rank, kept silence. Boubares sighed heavily and
stirred, conveying an impatience too great for sitting still.
"Must we wait forever?" he burst out. "They'll scatter
like dust before a storm when we fall on."

Metiochos got up. After all, he could not talk to Boubares. He took his leave and went inland between the
marsh and the rocky promontory which projected into the
sea to shelter the harbor. Here on the trampled turf the
horses and baggage animals were grazing. Metiochos
made the servants bridle his horse and crossed the

north of the plain in the direction of Marathon and the farm where he and his father and all their fathers had been born. Since the whole plain had long been deserted by terrified farmers, he met no living soul. From the damage to trees by axe and fire, or from trampled vineyards, it was clear that the cavalry had ranged across it.

In Marathon, the house looked smaller, as houses will after a long absence. Fire had gutted it. The great gates were battered down. Inside lay dirt and desolation. Charred fragments showed how beds and other objects had been piled in the court and set alight. Some of the timbers of the roof had caught fire and fallen in, but elsewhere the dingy rooms stood empty, waiting for their owners. Metiochos, though he had often thought of his unpretentious beginnings, was astonished to see how drab and primitive they were.

He went out of the empty house past other buildings huddled around an irregular square which used to be the exercise place until Aristias insisted that a town which bred Olympic victors needed a better one. There was a silence everywhere. The busy sparrow, the shouting lark, the calling rooks in the tall poplars had left with the people. Even the bees had deserted the blackened grass. Metiochos sat down with his back turned to his old home and he looked at the sea, a line in the distance. On his left lay the Persian camp and on his right the Athenian, both partly revealed by the cutting of the trees which had dotted the plain.

He did not waste time in wondering whether he was fated to die in this battle. If all his dreams and visions meant no more than this, why he was a soldier and had faced death before. Nor did it enter his mind to ride over into the Athenian camp, as Cleon had urged him. What good would he do by exposing all his kindred to the vengeance of Hippias and the wrath of Darius? Besides, he felt a duty in the matter. When he entered his captivity, he had died to his old life. Willingly he had snatched at a chance to start another. He had served the Great King gladly, catching from the Persians something of their chivalry. He had been useful in Bactria. He was the King's man. He was even Phaedime's husband.

What troubled him was a persistent feeling that the fate of the battle lay in his hands. Why it should do so, he could not yet see; but the future of Athens depended upon him. He was kin to Hippias, and to Miltiades. He could rule if he wanted to, like the governor in Sardis, listening to the Athenians as he pleased and granting power to them. He had done this in Bactria, and his rule had been good. But Bactria was dull. The coastal cities were vital and alive. They were even flourishing in a sort of way under Persian government. What good was freedom if all it meant was petty jealousy between states ridiculously small? He could not answer such a question, but he remembered the stricken silence in the throne room and the dusty people of Sestos waiting outside to hear that the Great King had taken it upon himself to enlarge his kingdom. Nothing had gone very well with Sestos since. The city had been too small a unit to be considered.

When it came to getting rid of unwanted tyrants, the Athenians had shown the way . . . for no reason except

that they at least were free to do so. The coastal cities had
needed to rebel and fight a war. Metiochos had not felt
at home in the new Athens, but he had listened to the
songs of Aeschylos admired the statue put up to those who
had slain Hippias's brother. He had noted how the great
names in Athens were no longer distinguished visitors
from abroad, but native men.

He looked out vaguely over the plain, accepting the fact
that he did not care for the cause which he must fight
for and that he might die at the hands of his own kin.
Let Zeus — or Ahura Mazda — dispose of his fate. Could
he as an Athenian have settled down to horse-breeding
or gossip in the marketplace? He did not think so. He
had been a wanderer instead, and he had seen much. Man
did not make his fate and could but endure it.

The sun was going down and presently would disappear
behind the hills, leaving a shadow to lengthen down the
plain toward the sea. Foragers were coming into the
Persian camp with food or fuel. Every so often he could
see the flash of the sun on shield or armor.

It was time for him to go, but he lingered, idly prolonging a calm that could not last amid the turmoil of an army.
He had not realized how far away one saw the gleam of
armor, nor how the angle of the sun magnified its size.
One could almost imagine that the glitter reflected an
army.

It took him another few seconds to comprehend that
Datis was sending his battle array out into the plain. The
actual movement was concealed by the marsh which,
rough with sedge, cut off his view. But in the portion of

the camp exposed to his eye, men in armor were forming into ranks. No doubt about it.

Metiochos sprang to his feet with such suddenness that
the corner of his eye caught a glimpse of movement behind a wall which used to protect a little vineyard from
the sheep and goats of its neighbors. Inwardly he cursed
himself for a fool. It stood to reason that the hills were
not really deserted. He had no business to ride out of
camp alone and sit here, offering his armor and his horses
as prizes to any who dared take them.

The thought had scarcely occurred to him before he
was over the wall against which he sat and crouching behind it while a stone whizzed perilously close to his head.
Metiochos instantly threw himself flat and rolled into a
depression at the foot of the low wall. Evidently assailants
had been creeping up from two directions, so that his
leaping across the wall had merely laid open his rear. Cautiously he tested this theory by raising the Bactrian felt
hat that he was wearing a bare six inches over his chest
on a stick. A slingshot crashed into it with such force that
he was lucky it did not also hit his hand. He let the hat
fall and lay still to think things over.

He had used a sling to hunt hares as a boy, and he knew
its accuracy and force at a close range. But much depended on selection of smooth stones and careful placing
of the missile in the leather sling. If you missed with the
first shot, it was not likely that the hare would still be
in range when you got off your second. Another drawback
to the weapon was the necessity of sweeping it in a wide
arc. Metiochos had not seen his assailant yet, for the sim-

ple reason that he had been in too much of a hurry to spare him a glance. But, remembering the complex of buildings and walls he understood exactly where the man must be and knew that he would step into the open when he had to give his weapon room.

He could not afford to wait while the second assailant on the other side of the wall crept closer to him or tried to steal his horse. If the hollow in which he lay had afforded enough cover, he could have wriggled along it to the corner, around which he would be able to watch both. Unluckily the ground flattened out, but it was possible that the slinger was not aware of this. Carefully cramping himself into the smallest possible space lest any of him betray his whereabouts, Metiochos brought knees up against his chest, secured a suitable missile from the loose stones under the wall, and clutched the useful stick in his left hand. Cautiously he slid this along the wall behind the grasses which grew at its foot, seeking a stone he could dislodge a yard away. He did not find this easy because he was half lying on that arm and had in any case no eyes to spare for what he was doing. Twice he caused a little rattle, but nothing happened. Sweat poured down his face. The Greek contingents would be filing onto the plain, and he not with them, nor likely to be unless he could guess the reactions of a man whom he had not so much as seen. Desperately he gave a stronger thrust and set a stone moving. As the sound broke the silence, he rose to his knees.

The slinger, distracted by the appearance of his enemy a fraction to the left of where he was aiming, missed both targets. Hastily he dodged back into hiding, avoiding a stone which Metiochos had thrown with far less force, but which he had selected because it was jagged.

Metiochos rose cautiously to his feet. Let the slinger so much as stick out his little finger, and he would discover how other people could throw stones.

In the exercise ground, his horse whinnied. Metiochos, backing down the wall, came to the corner where he could have a view. The second rustic, encumbered by a long stick pointed with iron, a common weapon among the wilder sort, was trying to catch at the bridle of his horse. The animal threw up his head and cantered away.

There was not much time to be lost. Metiochos discouraged the slinger from appearing with a couple of well-aimed stones, and he raced down the wall to head the animal off. He did not fear the man with the stick, who was misshapen, as so many of these goatherds were, with twisted legs under a heavy body. At close quarters he might be formidable, but Metiochos had not time to waste in fighting. He clicked his tongue at the horse and called to it in Aramaic, bringing it gently to a halt. Unbuckling his sword as he ran, he dropped it in the dust and, unencumbered, took a running leap which so startled the creature that they were fairly away before his hand was on the bridle. Mane and tail flying, they went thundering down the plain toward the sea, where the mass of Datis's army was beginning to debouch from the narrow passage between the coastline and the great marsh. Metiochos headed for the center of the bay to cut it off.

The message for which he had been waiting had come

to Datis about the time that Metiochos rode out of camp. Its nature, however, was such that his headquarters were thrown into a turmoil of angry confusion.

The partisans of Hippias had not risen, nor would they dare to do so, considering their numbers, unless the Persian were at the gates. Accordingly they had sent messages three days ago, imploring Datis to detach a force to sail round Attica and land in the bay of Phaleron. Frantically they had awaited some answer, and now they sent warning that they could not remain in readiness much longer. Notwithstanding, they would hold together for the present, provided Datis could detain the citizen army on Marathon plain.

Datis raged, but his reproaches had no effect on Hippias, save to confuse him and deprive the general of his advice. By temperament, Datis was a cautious man, used to crushing his enemies by immensely superior numbers. He did not relish dividing his forces. Besides, he had landed at Marathon and enticed the Athenians onto the open plain with the intention of breaking up their masses with cavalry. But it was precisely the cavalry which were certain to be needed for a dash up to the city from Phaleron It was true that even without his cavalry, Datis outnumbered the Athenian host. He still had the archery which so often had broken up Greek masses. Artaphernes, who wanted the glory of capturing Athens, could not imagine why Datis made a fuss about a maneuver which was not a danger but an opportunity.

Argument swayed back and forth, though actually Datis dared not throw away the chance to take Athens without a laborious siege. As Artaphernes pointed out, the enemy need never guess the cavalry was missing. Embarking at night and getting over the horizon before the sun came up, they could make a wide circle, landing at Phaleron and rushing the city in the early hours of the next dawn. Thereafter, some of them at least could jingle back up the coast road by which the Athenians had marched to Marathon plain.

Datis shook his head. Miltiades commanded the end of that coast road. By it, he could send a detachment to Athens more quickly than ships could sail clear around Attica. At any moment a message from the city might warn the Athenian army that treachery was planned.

The long discussion ate up the afternoon. Artaphernes was of the opinion that Datis should move out of the shelter of the marsh to draw up his army in battle line with his back to the south beach and left wing resting near the end of the coastal road. Then if Miltiades desired to send assistance to Athens, he would have to fight a battle, since the hill path was notoriously unfit for the movement of troops. "Meanwhile, by breaking up our camp and bringing ships to the south beach, we may cover the bustle of embarking our cavalry," he added.

Datis unwillingly agreed. So far the Athenians had shown no disposition to fight, and it was not probable that they would move out of their lines to challenge his army as long as they did not know his force was divided. Their tactic evidently was to wait for the Spartans.

The order for these movements was given in the late afternoon, and cheering ran through the soldiers' ranks.

Battlewise, the captains of tens shook their heads. The Athenians had no spirit. It would not come to a fight so easily. But even the captains showed a grim satisfaction in going forward.

The captains of tens proved perfectly right. The Athenians kept close inside their camp and made no movement while the glittering battle line was formed a mile away. By the time the last soldier was rigid in his place, the shadows of evening had crept down to the sea, and sentries were being posted. The formations began to loosen and break up as the soldiers, spreading out to get more room, took off their helmets, laid down their shields, and stuck their spears beside them. They all carried bread and handfuls of olives or raisins, so that they made their evening meal, while the camp servants brought water and wine from ships which had come over to draw up behind them on the beach. Men wrapped themselves in cloaks and lay down beside their armor. Those more wakeful moved together in small groups and grumbled. There still would be no battle.

Metiochos had joined the Greek contingents as they came onto the open plain. He had ridden with them, sending people back to fetch his servants and armor. In the bustle of so many movements, he had no sight of either until the ranks were settling down, and he discovered that his men had cleared a space for him a few yards to their rear. They had provided a bed of reeds from the marsh and a meal which they thought befitting the dignity of their commander. Metiochos, peering at it in the failing light, was a trifle shocked. He laughed abruptly.

"Never fight with a bloated belly! Take it away and tell Cleomenes to bring me bread and cheese. I'm going out into the plain to place my sentries in person!"

He did not need to give Cleon instructions. He simply took him on his rounds, exploring every gorse bush and stone wall which still encumbered the devastated plain. At points of vantage, he dropped off members of his escort, impressing on them the need to keep a lookout. "There are watchers on the hills, and if Miltiades learns from them the cavalry's gone, he'll attack. It is his chance. Watch well, I say."

Three times he made this pronouncement, never looking to see if Cleon were still at his heels. The moon was not yet up, and all the bustle which he himself was making served to cover the departure of one man. He did not hear or see it happen, but at the fourth point where he stopped and looked around, the slave Cleon was no longer with him. Now it only remained to be sure his absence was not noticed. This was easy. Metiochos soon went back to check over the straps of his armor. He did not feel like sleep. They said Miltiades was powerful with the senior Athenian general. Cleon would be persuasive, but councils of war were chancy things. Metiochos thought he had done what he was born for, what was fated for him many years back. The rest of it lay in the hands of the gods, of Zeus and the Wise One, Ahura Mazda, the invisible. Let them see to it.

The Battle

THE BATTLE LINE of the Athenians came out of their camp at first light. They must have set servants to tugging aside their brushwood screen while the men formed up inside. Before the half-light had revealed the openings to the Persian sentries, two close columns eight men across were emerging at a quick step which must have seemed like a run to men in brazen corselets, great, stuffy visored helmets, and heavy shields. Before the alarm had fairly been given, the two columns were separating, spreading out in an inverted V which grew wider and wider as more men poured through the central openings.

Horns sounded the alarm. In the Persian army many men were still asleep, while those who were awake had not put on their armor. In theory, the troops were encamped in line of battle; but in practice the need for elbow room, some casual visiting, and answering the calls of nature had created confusion. Nevertheless, this mattered little. The Athenian columns needed time to emerge, extend their line, and advance for a full mile. The Persian army might feel disorganized and out of breath; but the bulk of its soldiers were veterans, while all had been blooded in Euboea and the Cyclades. It was not taken by surprise, although it was hurried.

Sun flooded the top of Pentelicos, but in the valley there was gray shadow still, not obscuring the oncoming wall of men, who were still rolling forward even as they moved sideways, trying to cover the width of the Persian line. Their V, though flattening, was never stretched right out, so that conflict would be joined in the wings before the center.

"They're mad!" Boubares exclaimed. The position of his thousand was in the center with the best troops. It was taking longer than it ought to get his men in position because of the nearness of Datis and his bodyguard. The messengers of the commander, riding through the swarming ranks, were a continual harassment. All the same, Boubares's troops were primarily bowmen, though armed with spear and sword for the close fighting. The oncoming plalanx, lapped shield against shield and man behind man, was unsupported by any light-armed troops. It presented a massive, moving target at which his soldiers could take unhurried shots without being distracted by a rain of missiles on their ranks.

Metiochos on the right wing was forming his Greeks eight deep into a phalanx which more or less matched the storm rolling against them. Shield locked against shield, the men were too heavily armored and closely packed to fight at all. Their function was to charge like one bronze mass and clash with the other. Metiochos had light-armed archers on his flanks whose loose formations were running forward to get in range. They would do some execution until they were rolled back, but that moving monster in bronze armor was coming too fast for them. Metiochos did not think his father's dispositions mad in the least.

He looked down the gathering ranks of his men. They were hurrying, but not eager. His Greeks would fight because the alternative was to be killed, but they had no appetite for it. He had little himself, but the moment was exciting.

The sky was lightening behind them. At any moment the sun would be up over the hills of Euboea. Persian arrows were flying fast. The Athenian center was barely in range, but on the wing Metiochos could see the oncoming wall quiver slightly as men dropped their shields and were either borne onward in the packed mass of their fellows or else tramped beneath the feet of those pushing behind. But though the phalanx quivered, it did not break up. It actually increased its pace to a lumbering run which sent the archers back in confusion, lest they be caught when Metiochos countercharged. They shredded away like mist from between the two armies. Metiochos could hear the Athenians yelling as they came on. He recognized the shields of his own tribe in the ranks which opposed them. Once he had carried one himself. Miltiades would be somewhere opposite, and Conon also. The moment had come to throw up his arm in the signal. The trumpets brayed out over the din as his men charged.

Boubares heard the fearful crash as the right wing collided in battle. A moment later it was followed by a similar sound on the left. His own men were shooting fast and hard. Their arrows were falling on the enemy's mass like dark rain. He could see their center plalanx being broken into small groups as two or three shields went down together, and the survivors closed up in one direction or another. This always happened when Greeks opposed their limited tactics to Persians. On this occasion, the center had been stretched thin in an effort to cover the length of the Persian line, so that the breakup of its forces was easier than usual. To be sure, the phalanx still came on, but there was no strength in it. They would not stand against unwounded troops. Boubares gave the signal, and they charged.

Whatever the state of the center, the Athenian wings were solid and packed even deeper than usual. They came on like thunder. Shield crashed against shield, and men in the front rank had shoulders broken by the force of the collision. Fainting from the pain, they could not drop underfoot, but were carried upright against their foes like human battering rans.

There was no stabbing yet. The lines were bending as here and there the grunting ranks pushed forward, while others next to them were driven back. At first the pattern was an irregular one. Presently small wedges developed as the Athenians with their heavier weight of men and greater desperation bored into the enemy's line. Now cavalry was needed to take the enemy in flank, but the cavalry was over the horizon with Artaphernes, sailing for Athens. Metiochos's wing bent and twisted as men in the back ranks threw their weight desperately where it was needed, blocking one hole, only to uncover another. Minutes passed, and the Athenian wedges widened, crowding the opposite line into separate units.

Now the Athenians were bursting through into the open where they could use their spears. Their leading ranks were turning to hack at the unarmored flanks of their opponents, still wedged too tight to move. In a very few moments, the whole aspect of the battle changed. Men were no longer pushing into the thick of the press, but trying to get out. Metiochos's battle line was shredding and dissolving. His men were throwing down their heavy shields and running for their lives. Those panic-stricken, who had no heart for the fight, made for the beach. Metiochos and a confused mass of struggling men were forced inward against the Persian center by the formation of the Athenian V, which came crashing after.

So little time had all this taken that the battle of the

center, which had been joined ten minutes later, was still in progress. To be sure, the veterans of the Persian line had little trouble in dashing through the Athenian phalanx, which was here weaker and had borne the brunt of the fire of the archers. Boubares, charging at the head of his men, was already halfway to the Athenian camp, where he was spearing the light-armed troops or slaves who had followed the battle and could not get out of the way. Datis, however, and the bulk of the army were not so far forward. They were scattered all over the central battlefield, fighting less in line than in clumps around groups they had surrounded.

Into this confusing scene the Athenian right wing crashed. Its heavy armor, superior to the Persian leather corselet, was designed especially for hand-to-hand fighting. The easterners, slung about with bows and quivers as well as shields and spears and swords, were equipped for a more flexible maneuver. Taken in flank, without their cavalry, their bowmen useless in the confusion, they were driven into a formless mass. Even so their resistance was stubborn for a time. Presently, however, the Athenian left wing, victorious also, came bursting through against the hard-pressed center. Then panic began.

Behind Boubares, his men were shredding away. He tried to rally them and turn back on the center, but his numbers were not great enough for the task. The Athenian rabble of porters, light-armed troops, and fugitives from the central battle line had taken heart. Their sticks and stones were crude but fairly effective against an enemy who was now trying to turn his back and fight in the other direction. Boubares, conspicuous on his horse like most of the commanders, was a natural target for missiles. Luckily for him his leather tunic was sewn with scales of iron, as was the cap he wore on his head. Crouching low and holding up his shield of wicker, he tried with yells and blows to form his men. There was blood on the torn trouser of his left leg, and blood from his nose dripped down moustache and beard.

The men would not stand. Cut off from the south beach by the charge of the Athenian wings, the broken center was streaming over the plain in the direction of the marsh and their old camp beside the north beach, where many of the ships were still drawn up. Unhorsed and borne along against his will, Boubares went with them while the Athenians, impeded by their heavier armor, pounded yelling after.

Swept along by the same irresistible movement, Datis was already far ahead of the battle, entering the narrow place where marsh and shore came close together. Here at last determined spirits who had not thrown their weapons away were facing about to make a stand. Datis rallied them, riding in person up to groups as they came by and challenging them to turn and fight. Among these the band of Athenian exiles thundered past him. Charmides, who was no coward in war, had taken Hippias before him on his horse because the old man could not any longer sit upright. The tyrant had sent his grandson with Artaphernes, preferring to make a triumphal entry himself when victory was won. Now he slumped against Charmides, mouth half open and head lolling, hardly con-

scious of confusion or defeat. There was blood on his
robe.

Pursuers and pursued rolled down in confusion on the
narrow spot where Datis stood at bay. Soon it was choked
with struggling men. The weaponless or the frightened
and the wounded who were trying to reach the ships were
blocked by Datis and the troops he had formed in line.
Wild panic followed. Men who had fought side by side
now struggled with each other, clawing a road to safety
over the bodies of those who had dropped exhausted.
Behind them, the Athenians, grimly butchering the
fringes of the crowd, drove it closer together.

It was everyone for himself now. Boubares was no
longer even with the men of his thousand. He was trying
with hundreds of people strange to him to get through
the marsh, but he was weighted with his armor and impeded by the flesh wound in his leg. The place was passable for an active boy who was lightly clad, but hardly for
a regiment of armored men with death behind them.
Boubares climbed out of mud and water onto a tussock
and stood a moment, wavering. There was a dazzle in
front of his eyes. Objects slid into one another. He was
conscious of the sound of his own breathing over the noises
all about him. With a vast effort he lifted a foot and tried
to move it forward, feeling about him aimlessly because
he could see nothing. Something struck him heavily in the
back, and he fell forward, face down in mud and water.
He did not get up, and other people used him as a stepping stone into the quagmire.

Meanwhile, the Greeks of the right wing streamed onto

the south beach. Those who had arrived early had been the cowards who had fled at the first breakthrough. It happened that the ships moved round to the south beach behind the army had been all Phoenician. The sailors had a low opinion of Greeks, their eternal rivals, and by no means welcomed the flood of men who, hardly trying to launch the ships from the beach, poured onto the gangways.

As long as the fugitives were only Greeks, the Phoenicians were not disposed to think the battle lost. It did not occur to them to put out to sea, especially as there had been little pursuit. Thus by the time the fighting men were driven back, both from the center and from the remains of Metiochos's wing, it was not easy to launch the ships at all, weighed down by people who were frightened to lose their place in them if they got out. This time the pursuit was close at men's heels. The Athenians came plunging to the edge of the surf, only to be driven back by a short rally which Metiochos directed himself.

The trouble was, he had to be everywhere. The men who were still fighting were too few to hold the Athenians back for long. Besides, they fought halfheartedly, constantly looking to be sure the ships had not pushed off and left them to be massacred where they stood. Meanwhile, around the ships themselves a few people who saw what ought to be done were vainly trying to push them down the sand. These, however, were too much hurried to form a team or to tackle one at a time. Conscious that they were exposing defenseless backs, they were as nervous as the fighters who were trying to protect them.

There was no time to be lost. What seemed like half the army was pouring onto the beach, which evidently would soon be so crowded with men that the Athenians could massacre at their leisure. Luckily because the distance was not great the number of soldiers who still had arms in their hands was considerably larger than it was around the marsh and the north beach. It was just possible to leave the fighting to those who could not push their way through to the water. Metiochos threw down his shield and spear to put his shoulder against the nearest ship, encouraging others by continuous cries to follow his example.

She slid into the water, and there was a furious struggle among everyone who was near to get aboard her. Men swept into the surf, pushing Metiochos waist-deep into the water. The sudden movement created a funnel-like hole in the crowd, and into it like avenging furies plunged the Athenians.

Metiochos stumbled, nearly carried under by the weight of his own breastplate. Suddenly his voice, which was hoarse and dry from shouting, had gone altogether. But some of the other ships were afloat, only just in time. That next to him slid by in the water, as an Athenian, stumbling to the water's edge a fraction ahead of his fellows, caught a trailing rope and pulled her up short. Someone cut it off, but the water was crowded with men being hoisted aboard, and they could not get the oars out. The Athenian — he was of Metiochos's own tribe — had his hand on the gunwale and was jabbing with his spear at a swordsman leaning out to swing at him.

The swordsman shrunk together, barely avoiding the thrust, and shortened his range to bring down his weapon on the Athenian's wrist. He severed it like a billet of wood on a chopping block. The Athenian gave a great cry and fell backward into the water, jerking his helmet off. It was Conon, Metiochos's dearest boyhood friend, whose sister he should have married. Conon's face was pale as ashes, and he looked already dead.

Metiochos had hardly time to feel a pang, though it crossed his mind that he and Conon had both heard ghostly sounds so long ago. Nearly all the ships were floating now. One or two of them had got oars out, and several were poling themselves into deeper water. But men were still skirmishing on the beach, men for whom there was no room in the ships, men whose resistance had made it possible for the rest to get away. They were the last remnants of his own contingents from the coast, the cream of his soldiers, who had looked to him to bring them safely home. Wading shoreward through the struggling crowd in the water, Metiochos went back to join them.

Epilogue

THE BATTLE was over by ten o'clock in the morning. Datis and his ships put out to sea, leaving behind him more than six thousand dead. His hopes, however, were not extinguished yet. The victorious army might still melt away if Artaphernes could take Athens.

Behind him on the field of battle, the Athenians took helmets off and sat down, most of them where they were. Many were wounded in unprotected arms or legs by the rain of arrows and had fought five hours notwithstanding. The Persian fugitives had thrown their heavy armor away, but the victors had pursued them over the plain in full bronze panoply through the heat of a summer day. Such of the servants as were not better employed in plundering brought skins of wine and water.

The Athenian soldiers looked around them taking in their victory and gazing with new pride of ownership at Marathon plain and the hills surrounding it. One or two of them noticed a flash of light on Pentelicos. It was gone in an instant, but came again. Whole groups were soon staring at it.

Miltiades and the War Leader, not to mention the eight other generals, had no doubts of its meaning. Uncertain whether their messages had ever reached the Persian, the friends of Hippias were signaling to him by flashing a shield in the sun. At last they were ready to betray Athens.

The town was twenty-six miles off, and the army was weary; but there was no time to be lost. The Athenians set out in the heat of the day to stumble back to Athens, upheld by the thought of the glorious deeds they had done. Thus when the leading Persian ships sailed into Phaleron, the ranks of their enemies, as grim as on the day before, stood ready to meet them.

Artaphernes hesitated. Datis, who soon followed, knew better than to try conclusions again. He drew off, not to the Cyclades, whose loyalty he did not trust in defeat, but to Lemnos, which had belonged to Miltiades once and now was Persian. Here he landed his sick, among them Hippias, who had spoken no word but incoherent mumbles since the day of Marathon. Here Hippias laid his bones at last, while the land of his fathers retained no more than his lost tooth.

The Great King, wise in war, was not ungenerous enough to reproach Datis. But the King grew old and twisted with rheumatism. Campaigning was impossible for him; while his lieutenants, left to themselves, had brought on disasters. The King did not renounce his claim to Greece, but it was noticed that his cupbearer no longer bade him remember the Athenians. He would let his son Xerxes, tall and handsome, have the glory of this conquest when the throne came to him. The Great King contented himself with his vast dominions.

Perhaps it might be that the loss of a single servant whom he had destined for great things was a disappointment. He did not say so, but he gave vast gifts to Phaedime's son, more than to the sons of Boubares or of other nobles who had died for him. Megabates was richly endowed, and he married nobly. A hundred and fifty years later, when Alexander the Greek conquered the Persian Empire, he married a princess in Bactria called Roxana, whose father was named Gergis and whose ancestor was Megabates.